A CRY FOR HELP

It was close to noon, plenty of time to grab a quick wink before picking up the kids. The rewrite on the novel could wait one more day. Brenna's problems could wait one more day.

Then the phone rang.

I picked it up and said. "Hello?"

I could hear someone having hysterics in the background. Screaming and crying. It was not a soothing sound. "Hello?" I shouted into the phone.

"E.J.! Oh God, E.J.?"

"Brenna? Is that you? What's going on?"

"Oh God, E.J.? Get over here quick! Something's happened to Lorabell! Something awful!"

The line went dead in my hands.

Other E.J. Pugh Mysteries by
Susan Rogers Cooper
from Avon Books

ONE, TWO, WHAT DID DADDY DO?
HICKORY DICKORY STALK
HOME AGAIN, HOME AGAIN

THERE WAS A LITTLE GIRL
AN E. J. PUGH MYSTERY

SUSAN ROGERS COOPER

AVON BOOKS ◆ NEW YORK

AVON BOOKS
A division of
The Hearst Corporation
1350 Avenue of the Americas
New York, New York 10019

Copyright © 1998 by Susan Rogers Cooper
Published by arrangement with the author
Visit our website at **http://www.AvonBooks.com**
Library of Congress Catalog Card Number: 92-94310
ISBN: 0-380-79468-3

First Avon Books Printing: March 1998

AVON TRADEMARK REG. U.S. PAT. OFF. AND IN OTHER COUNTRIES, MARCA REGIS-
TRADA, HECHO EN U.S.A.

Printed in the U.S.A.

WCD   10 9 8 7 6 5 4 3 2 1

For Evin Cooper,
who has taught me all the highs,
and a few of the lows, of parenting.

Acknowledgments

I would like to thank all those who helped in the process of this book. A special thanks to Judith Miller, M.S.W., for her insights into the human psyche; to Barbara Burnett Smith and Don Cooper, for reading and critiquing the manuscript; and a very special thank you to my agent Vicky Bijur, and my editor Ann McKay Thoromon, for their confidence and encouragement.

One

There's one thing positive I can say about Christmas vacation: It's not as long as summer vacation. We were on the downhill side, coming—oh, so slowly—up to New Year's, the second day of which was *back-to-school day*! That has a nice ring to it, doesn't it?

My three kids were in the backseat of the station wagon as we headed to Grandma's house, Graham, my almost-ten-year-old, in the middle, flanked by his two six-year-old sisters.

As the babble grew louder, I looked in the rearview mirror, only to see Bessie with her hand on the seat-belt release.

"Stay in your seat belt!" I said.

"I can't hit Graham on top of the head if I have to stay in my seat belt," Bessie answered reasonably.

"Don't hit your brother," I said, deftly maneuvering around a pothole in the highway.

"He hit me!" Bessie reasoned.

"Stay in your seat belt. Graham, don't hit your sister."

"Which one?" Graham asked.

"Either one!" I said. Okay, I shouted.

"Look! A wreck!" Graham said.

In the northbound lane, the one I would eventually be taking back home, there was indeed a wreck.

"Cool!" Megan, my other six-year-old, said. "See any bodies?"

"Naw," Graham said.

All three were out of their seat belts in a flash, noses pressed against the left-side window of the car, peering out at the carnage, or lack thereof.

"Get back in your seat belts and stop staring," I said. "You little ghouls. That's terribly uncool, you know."

They all ignored me, which was what I would have done had my mother said those words to me. Of course, my mother would never have said "cool."

Finally we pulled into my mother-in-law's driveway with doors flying open, kids flying out, and dogs flying down the steps. Vera leaned against the porch post and looked at me, her arms folded across her chest.

"I'm gonna start charging you," she said.

"Any amount would be gladly given," I answered. "I'll even take a second mortgage out on the house."

When my two daughters ran up to her for a hug, she seemed to forget about the phantom money. I kissed the appropriate cheeks and shook the appropriate hand and hightailed it back to the car, heading to Black Cat Ridge, the subdivision where I lived, and where I was expected to chair an auction for the fledgling community battered women's center in less than thirty minutes.

Black Cat Ridge is almost a small city unto itself. We have our own elementary and middle schools, a fairly new high school, a fire substation, grocery-store chains, drugstores, etc., making the need to cross the Colorado River into Codderville almost unnecessary—for those who can find baby-sitters within the community.

Unfortunately, I am not one of the chosen. When new

families with teenagers move in, we can usually get one to sit—once; but with the Pugh family, unlike Jacqueline Susann, once appears to be more than enough. My mother-in-law Vera takes up more than slack.

Remembering the wreck in the northbound lane, I headed for the back road, Old Brenham Highway, which crossed the river a mile upstream.

It was winter in central Texas. We don't get snow here. We get rain and temperatures that vary between zero and ninety degrees, sometimes, not often but sometimes, in the same day. This day, the third day before the new year, it was forty degrees at 9 A.M., but the sun was shining brightly and there was a good chance we'd make it to seventy before the sun set.

I'd stayed off this old road since I'd almost been killed on the banks under the bridge the year before, but my fear of bad traffic was as intense as my memories.

The sun glinted off the waters of the Colorado River (the Texas Colorado River—not to be confused with that *other* Colorado River in that *other* state) when I noticed something out of whack.

The bluish brown water, the beige sandy banks of the river, the green and brown of the trees, and the white of the bridge made the pink of the party dress stand out like a roach in a Tupperware drawer.

I slowed the car and pulled to the side of the bridge. There was a girl standing on the other side—the *wrong* side—of the railing, her body facing the water below, her arms behind her hanging on to the bridge rail. The pink party dress was stained and her abundance of dark hair was in day-after disarray—some still pinned up in its formerly fancy do, other strands hanging limply around her face.

I got out of the car and walked slowly toward the girl poised on the bridge. In one hand holding on to the bridge rail were a pair of cheap gold-and-silver sandal-type party shoes. She turned her face toward me, and I could see she was no more than fifteen or sixteen years old. Mascara stained her face in streaks, and too much blush pocked her face in splotches.

She was smaller than me, maybe five-five to my five-eleven, and thin. From the bodice of the outdated pink party dress I could see the edges of Kleenex peeking through.

"Hi," I said, doing my perky cheerleader greeting.

"Go away!" she screamed.

Okay, I thought, *so we're not going to play perky cheerleader.*

"I mean it! Stay away from me!" she shouted.

I stopped on the road, putting my hands up in front of me like a traffic cop. "Don't," I said. "Please."

"Go away! Leave me alone!"

I took a quick gulp of air. "I'm E.J.," I said, trying to make my voice as neutral as possible. "What's your name?"

It had been thirteen years since my training as a volunteer for Houston's Crisis Hotline, but it was a little like riding a bicycle—the procedures were coming back to me in flashes. *Keep your voice calm. Say your name and ask theirs.*

"Get away!"

"I'm not coming any closer, I promise," I said, standing my ground. "I just want to talk to you." *Be firm yet gentle.*

"I don't want to talk! Go away!"

"Please," I said. "It can't be that bad—" *Don't belittle their feelings*—oops.

"How the hell do you know how bad it is?"

"Please just talk to me. Maybe I can help." *Be their friend—their lifeline.*

She laughed and snorted at the same time, tears streaming down her face. I was worried the tears were blinding her and she'd reach out to wipe them away. If she did that, she would surely fall.

"I'm E.J.—" *Repeat your name when necessary.*

"I don't care who you are!"

"I want to help you." *Show your concern without pushing.*

"I'm way past helping," she whined. "Nobody can help me anymore!"

"Please let me try," I said, shuffling slowly toward her.

"Get back!" she shouted.

I stopped in my tracks. "I won't move any closer, I promise," I said, knowing it was a promise I would break in a heartbeat. *Lie, cheat, steal. Just keep them alive.* "Just let me talk to you."

The girl sighed heavily. "Please tell my grandma I love her," she said, then let go of the railing.

In the two years I'd worked as a Hotline volunteer, I'd never lost one. Maybe it wasn't like riding a bicycle after all.

I stood transfixed; the scene before me moved like a film in slow motion. The gold-and-silver sandals dangled for a while from one finger, then escaped, the sun glinting off the metallic splendor as they fell, along with the girl's body, into the waters of the Colorado.

I knew the river at this section. We'd had rain lately, and this was a deep section. The bridge was no higher, really, than the high board at the local swimming pool. If she could swim, she'd make it.

Her body hit with a small splash, and she was under. The currents were strong here. I ran to the other side of the bridge. Her head popped up, and she screamed, "I can't swim!"

Well, shit! I thought. I stripped off my down jacket and my Reeboks, climbed the side of the railing and jumped, not giving much thought to what I was doing. Which was probably a good thing. Thought might have stopped me. This move had definitely *not* been in the Hotline handbook.

The water was icy—so cold I felt the goose bumps rising all over my body and felt my teeth begin to chatter. *Swim,* I told myself. *Swim fast.*

She was in front of me, head bobbing in and out of the

water, spitting the water out of her mouth as she tried to scream. Obviously not a lot of thought had gone into her plan either.

In four long strokes, with the help of the current and her inability to swim, I caught up with her. She grabbed my hair and tried to climb on top of my head, pushing me under the water. Luckily I had weight and knowledge on my side. I grabbed her, slapped her sharply in the face, said, "Be still!" and pulled her to the bank of the river in a fairly easy lifeguard move I'd learned in Girl Scouts twenty-five years before.

I yanked her up the bank, and we both lay there panting, exhausted and freezing.

Finally, she said, "Who the hell are you and why are you butting into my life?"

"I'm E.J. Pugh and I'm not butting into your life, honey, I'm butting into your death."

She rolled away from me and started to rise. Too tired to get up and follow her if she ran, I just grabbed the soaked party dress and pulled. She plopped down beside me.

"Let go!" she said.

I shook my head, too exhausted to do much more. "Where did you think you were going?"

"I'm cold," she whined. "I dunno. Just away from here." She began to cry, large choking sobs that racked her thin body.

We were both lying on the ground, the girl's back to me. I moved to her, putting my arms around her and hugging her, hoping some of my own body heat would reach her.

I'm not a professional shrink. I'm not even much of an amateur one. But I am a mom—how good a mom my children might debate. I could only do what I knew worked with my kids. I held her and began to sing softly in her ear. I'm about as good a singer as I am a shrink, but she began to calm down.

We lay that way for what felt like hours, but was probably not more than ten or fifteen minutes.

"Why are you doing this?" she finally asked.

"Because I don't want you to die," I said.

"You don't even know me!"

"What difference does that make?" I asked her.

Releasing her, although still holding her hand, I sat up, and said, "I have to call someone for you."

She shook her head. "No one to call," she said.

"I think I should take you to the emergency room, let them look you over."

She tried to pull out of my grip. "No!" she said.

"I'll stay with you," I said. "I won't let anything happen to you."

She was silent for a moment, and then she said, "Promise?"

This was a promise I had no intention of breaking.

I used my cell phone to call the women's center to let them know I wasn't going to make it to the auction—although they'd probably figured that out by now since I was over an hour late.

I now had a cell phone—real nineties' kinda gal, that's me. We got the cell phone *after* my husband was lost for almost a week; just like we got caller ID *after* we'd had threatening phone calls, and just like we got an alarm system for the house *after* someone had broken in and almost killed the entire family. We, my husband Willis and I, are very good at hindsight.

The intern in the ER was checking the girl out while a nurse wrapped me in a blanket.

"You need to get out of those wet clothes," she said. "Go home and take some Extra Strength Tylenol."

"And hot chocolate," I said. "I think this definitely calls for hot chocolate."

She smiled. "And a dollop of rum, if I were you," she said as she walked off.

I went to the waiting room to play with my cell phone. This time I dialed the number of Anne Comstock, the therapist who'd helped our family through a few crises.

After I explained the situation, Ann said, "I'm not taking any new patients right now, E.J., and besides, we don't know if the girl's indigent or not. What kind of insurance she has. Sorry for being practical, but there it is."

"Anne, I realized you didn't do this for fun after the third or fourth session," I said. "Can you recommend someone?"

"Yeah," she said. I could hear the flutter of her Rolodex, then she said, "There's a new program that just started up last month. Sliding scale mostly, but they do take some indigent patients." She gave me a number. "Josh Morgan's the director and maybe the only counselor working right now. Like I said, they're very new. But, from what I've heard, he's good."

I thanked her and hung up, dialing the number she gave me. A woman answered, and I explained the situation. Not knowing the girl's name, I made the appointment for later that day under my own name and made my way back to the white-curtained cubicle where the girl was.

I stuck my head in, and said, "Hi."

She was lying on the bed, which was slanted upward to an almost-sitting position, covered in blankets, the ruined party dress in a heap on the floor. The young intern sat in a chair by her side, a clipboard in hand.

He looked up at me. "Can I help you?" he said.

The girl said, "She's the one who saved my life."

The intern said, "Can I help you?"

Overwhelmed by his show of community gratitude and good cheer, I said, "Just checking on her."

"Why don't you wait in the waiting room?" he suggested.

"E.J.? Please stay," the girl said.

The intern shrugged, and I sat down at the foot of the bed.

"Okay, I'm almost through here anyway," he said. "I've got a psych consult on the way."

"Why?" I asked.

"Because she tried to commit suicide," the intern said, his voice dripping with sarcasm.

"I meant," I said, enunciating precisely, "what would this consult accomplish?"

"She won't give us her name or her next of kin. She's obviously underage—"

"I'm eighteen," the girl said.

"—and she tried to commit suicide, so the psych consult will need to make the decision on having her committed—"

"Committed!" the girl shrieked.

"Let me talk to her a moment, okay?" I asked the intern.

He shrugged and pushed the button on the end of his ballpoint—a gesture of finality. "Whatever," he said, and left the cubicle.

"You said I'd be okay!" she screamed. "Now they're going to commit me—"

She was struggling to get off the bed. I pushed her back down and kept my hand on her chest, holding her there. "Where are your parents?" I asked. "You have to give us something, honey. You can't just expect these people to release you to the streets!"

"Why not? They do it all the time! I saw this movie about this girl who goes to New York City and—"

"This isn't New York City, honey. This is a small-town America. Worse: Small-town Texas. They're not going to just let an underage girl who tried to commit suicide walk out the door. Where are your parents?"

She shrugged. "I don't have any," she finally said.

I gave her a look.

"I haven't seen my father since I was three," she said.

"And your mother?" I asked.

She turned her eyes away from me and shrugged.

"You said something about your grandmother," I said, remembering her last words before she jumped off the bridge.

"I live with her," she said, her voice a whisper.

"Is your grandmother your legal guardian?" I asked.
She shrugged again. "Yeah, I guess."

"What don't we call her?" I asked.

The girl snorted a laugh. "Oh, yeah, let's call Grandma!
That's gonna help."

"She's your legal guardian, honey. What's your first
name so I can stop calling you honey?"

She smiled. The first smile I'd seen from her. "I dunno,
I kinda like honey."

I smiled back. "Shall I fill that out on the hospital
forms?"

"Brenna," she said.

I smiled. "That's a pretty name," I said.

"It sucks."

"What's your last name?" I asked.

She gave me a sidelong glance. "You're trying to
trick me."

"Okay, fine. Don't tell me your last name. I'll come
visit you in whatever institution they put you in."

"McGraw. Brenna McGraw. My grandmother's name
is Millie Conrad, and she lives at—"

"Whoa!" I said, grabbing for my purse and some paper.
"Let me write this down."

Millie Conrad was a piece of work and then some. She
was probably in her early sixties, but looked older. Four-
foot-eleven, she weighed maybe eighty pounds, wore
makeup thicker than Tammy Faye in her prime, had several prominent teeth missing, and chain-smoked—to the
chagrin of the hospital staff who were continually telling
her to put out her cigarette—which she dutifully did, and
then would immediately light another. It took the threat
of the maximum state fine for smoking in a nonsmoking
establishment for her to stop. And then she had to hand
her cigarettes and lighter to Brenna to hide them from her.

And she talked. She talked from the minute she walked
in and didn't stop to take a breath, much less let someone
else speak.

"My God, my God, Brenna, what have you done? Did you get drunk at that party? Drugs? Is that it? Did you take drugs at that party?"

"Grandma—"

" 'Cause if you did, I'm gonna sue somebody, I'll tell you that much!"

"Mrs. Conrad—" I started.

"You'd think some parents don't have a lick of sense! Having parties where children can get drunk and take all sorts of dope! Your hair's a mess! I been up all night worrying about you! Why didn't you call me? I woulda come got you no matter what time! Haven't I told you a thousand times that if somebody lights up one of them reefers, you call me—"

"Grandma, I didn't do any dope—"

"—that you was to call me and I'd come get you and give him a piece of my mind! Why would you try to kill yourself, honey? That's a mortal sin—"

"We're not Catholic—"

"All I know is what I read in the Good Book, and it tells me that killing yourself is an abomination unto the Lord God His ownself, and I'm just so damned glad you're okay I could just cry!"

Whereupon she did. Cry, that is. Which didn't seem to stop the flow of words in the least.

Trying again, I said, "Mrs. Conrad—"

"Nurse, honey, could you get me a tissa?" She squeezed my arm. "There's a doll," she said, then turned back to Brenna. "Everything in your life is getting ready to turn up rosy and you go and do a fool thing like this and I could just scream is what I could do—"

"Grandma, she's not a nurse."

"Who's not a what, honey?"

Brenna pointed at me. "This is the lady who saved my life."

Silence ensued for about an entire five seconds. Then Millie Conrad, all four feet, eleven inches of her, grabbed me by the middle and hugged me tight. I'm used to being taller than most women, but patting Mrs. Conrad's back felt like patting one of my children.

"You are an angel is what you are," Millie Conrad said, leaning away to look up into my face, her tiny hands still on my ample hips. "God sent you down to protect my little baby girl and His will be done, praise the Lord—"

"I was just in the right place at the right—" I tried.

"I'll cook you my famous chili is what I'm gonna do. You like chili, nurse lady? 'Cause that's what—"

"Grandma, she's not a nurse!" Brenna shouted.

Millie Conrad let go of me and turned to her grand-daughter. "Well, you don't have to get huffy with me, young lady." The tears started flowing again. "I done what I could with you when your mama went away. I tried everthing I knew to bring you up to be a good Christian young lady, and then you blaspheme like all get-out going and doing something like this here and all I can say is, Lord have mercy, I tried, I really, really did—"

"Grandma, I know, I'm sorry, all I'm saying is—"

"My name's E.J. Pugh," I said, holding out my hand. "I don't work for the hospital, Mrs. Conrad. I was just driving by and—"

"So you work for one of them private doctors then?" she asked.

"Grandma, she's not a nurse!"

"Then why did you tell me she was?" Mrs. Conrad asked.

Brenna just looked at me and shrugged. And I wondered why it had taken the child sixteen years to try to jump off a bridge.

Two

"**You did what?**" Willis said, his face turning an interesting shade of puce. Normally, Willis is a rather good-looking fella, at least I've always thought so. He's big and blond and brown-eyed and fits me like a glove. I just wasn't sure I liked the new look of his complexion.

"Honey, it was no big—achoooooo—"

"My God, you've caught pneumonia."

"It must be my sinuses. The army did an experiment where they wet down soldiers and stuck them outside in low temperatures to prove that wet and temperature have nothing to do with catching colds." I sneezed again, this time so hard my head flew to my knees. I almost made contact.

"Where do you get these facts?" Willis said, his voice rising.

"I web it sombwew—" I grabbed a Kleenex from the box on the kitchen counter and blew my nose. "I read it somewhere. Personally, I thought it was rather cruel."

"You're trying to get me off track—"

"Okeb," I said. I blew my nose again. "What would you have done under similar circumstances?"

"Did you ever think of using the cell phone and calling the cops?" he asked, his voice that serious soft tone he uses when he's trying to be reasonable against all odds.

"Oh," I said. We hadn't had the phone *that* long. "Well, they wouldn't have gotten there in time."

He shook his head and looked around the house. "Where are my children?" he asked.

Okay, now they were *his* children. *That* didn't happen often. Maybe I could take advantage of it. "At your mother's."

"You forgot to pick up the children?" he asked, like it was something I did on a weekly basis. Admittedly, I thought about forgetting them at Vera's often, but I've never done it. And it wasn't like I'd done it now.

I'd called Vera from the hospital, telling her what had happened. Unlike her oldest son, she had been sympathetic to not only "that poor little darlin' girl," but to me as well.

When the psychiatrist showed up for the consult, I explained about the appointment I'd set up for the girl later that day. He asked her a few questions in front of both her grandmother and me, then signed her discharge orders, agreeing that Josh Morgan was a proper referral.

Millie Conrad's car was in the shop that day, and she'd gotten a ride to the hospital from a neighbor who had just dropped her off. I got the pleasure of taking Brenna and her grandmother home.

I was cold, wet, and grumpy as I listened to Mrs. Conrad's constant chatter on the fifteen-mile trip to the tiny community of Swamp Creek. Brenna sat in the backseat, and, every time I glanced in the rearview mirror, I got the feeling she was regretting my efforts on her behalf.

There's an old Chinese proverb that says if you save a life, you become responsible for it. I was beginning to feel very responsible. I'd told her she had something to live for. What if I'd been wrong?

Following Mrs. Conrad's detailed instructions, I only got lost twice before we pulled into the driveway of their home. It was a tiny, gingerbread-looking house, and I couldn't help thinking my daughters would love to have one like it in the backyard.

Swamp Creek was on the Black Cat Ridge side of the Colorado River, and the few teenagers the town boasted went to the Black Cat Ridge High School. I asked Brenna what grade she was in, and she said she was a junior. I still had a few contacts at the school, left over from my friendship with my daughter Bessie's birth sister Monique, and I thought I'd do some checking.

I told Mrs. Conrad about Brenna's appointment that afternoon with Josh Morgan.

"Well, there's no way I can get her back into Codderville. My car's in the shop."

"Don't worry about it, E.J.," Brenna said from the backseat. "I'll change the appointment."

"No," I said. "Don't change it. I'll pick you up at three o'clock."

"You don't have to do—" Brenna started.

"The psychiatrist let you out of the hospital on the condition that you keep this appointment, Brenna. This wouldn't be a good way to begin the relationship."

"I don't know what we'd do without you, Nurse E.J.," Mrs. Conrad said, getting out of the car.

"Grandma, she's not a nurse!"

I touched Brenna's hand. "Don't worry about it. I'll see you at three."

Because of my cold and wet condition, I'd opted to go straight home rather than back across the river to pick up the kids. I'd been looking up the phone number for Wendy Beck, Monique's best friend, when my husband had come through the door.

Since he was three hours earlier than he was supposed to be, I thought the question as to the whereabouts of his children had been a test. I think he knew precisely where they were, and he also knew precisely what had happened that morning. Obviously Vera had called him and given him the details. He just wanted to see how much I'd actually tell him. You'd think after as many years as we'd been together there'd be a little trust, for God's sake.

"I have to go back into Codderville to take Brenna to counseling," I said. "I'll pick up the kids then."

He said, "Goddamnit!"

I had been sitting at the breakfast table, my face in my cup of tea, hoping the steam would open my sinuses. His expletive made me jump, spilling the tea on the table.

"What?" I said, matching his voice in anger.

"You coulda been killed!"

"Well, I wasn't!"

"Yeah, but you could have been!"

"Yeah, but I wasn't!"

"How stupid *are* you?"

I stood up and drew my woolly robe around. "I married you, didn't I?" I shot back.

We stood there glaring at each other. In my heart I knew this was a fear fight—he'd been afraid for me, which made him angry. I can be rational. I can understand these things. That didn't mean I had to put up with it.

Willis slammed out the back door and stood on the patio, glaring at the backyard. I could see him from the window of the breakfast room. I sat back down and sniffed my tea some more. I had my cold-fighting team in front of me: camomile tea, vitamin C, and zinc lozenges. I took a handful of the vitamins and the lozenges and started chewing. Then I looked at the clock. It was two-thirty. I had half an hour to get dressed and pick up Brenna. I went to the back door and opened it.

"I'm going upstairs to get dressed," I told my husband's back. "I have to get the girl to counseling."

He turned around. "Why do *you* have to get this kid to counseling?"

"Because her grandmother's car's in the shop," I said reasonably.

"And that's the only person in this girl's life, right?" he asked.

"Maybe so. Do you think she tried to kill herself for kicks?"

That remark got me Willis's back again. I closed the back door and headed for the stairs.

Unfortunately Millie Conrad thought it was only proper that she ride to Josh Morgan's office with Brenna and me. I couldn't really disagree. She was, after all, the girl's legal guardian.

I couldn't help noticing Brenna's clothes as the two got in the station wagon. Her polyester "silk look" blouse was two sizes too big and in a color I hadn't seen around in almost a decade. She wore this over a straight, black skirt that hung to mid-calf and billowed out at the hips.

Two minutes after getting into the car, Millie Conrad started fanning herself. "I think I'm taking one of my spells," she said, her voice whispery.

I looked in the backseat at Brenna, who rolled her eyes. I wondered if this was just teenage disregard for other people or a sign that Mrs. Conrad's "spells" were legendary in the family.

"Are you all right, Mrs. Conrad?" I asked.

She thrust her arm at me. "Feel my pulse, Nurse. I think my heart's exploding."

"Grandma, your heart's not exploding," Brenna said from the backseat, her voice resigned.

"How could it not with what you been doing to it, little girl?" her grandmother said, whirling around in the seat in a very healthy fashion. She whirled back to me. "We walk in the house while go and what do you think she done? Well, I'll tell you what she done. She went straight to her room and closed and locked that door and didn't answer me for nothing. That's what she done. I begged and I pleaded, but she wouldn't open the door at all! And me being hypoglycemic and all!"

"Grandma, you're not hypoglycemic—"

"You know anybody has to eat as often as I do just to stay alive who ain't hypoglycemic? Tell me that, little girl. You just tell me that!"

In the rearview mirror I could see Brenna's arms crossing her chest and her chin raised in defiance. "Well, all I know, *old* woman, is hypoglycemics don't eat chocolate eighteen hours a day!"

Millie Conrad twisted sharply in the seat and reached out a short arm and slapped Brenna soundly on the face.

I pulled the car over to the side of the road.

Mrs. Conrad was yelling, "Don't you call me old woman!" while Brenna was screaming, "Then don't call me little girl!" as I slammed on the brakes and turned off the engine. With the silence of the engine, both stopped and looked at me. I stared daggers at Mrs. Conrad.

"Don't ever hit her again," I said.

"You got no right—"

"You don't slap a child in the face. I don't care what your child-rearing methods are, you don't slap a child in the face!"

Brenna was sitting in the backseat with a smug look on her face. I turned on her. "And you, young lady, *do not* show such disrespect to your grandmother!" I took a deep breath. "Look, I'm going out of my way to help you two. I don't know either of you from Adam, but I'm trying to be a good citizen, you understand? But if either of you tries this kinda shit again, I'm leaving you on the side of the road. Are you both perfectly clear on my meaning here?"

"Well, you don't have to get huffy—" Mrs. Conrad started.

"Grandma—"

I sat in stony silence until they both looked a little crestfallen. "Okay," Brenna said. Mrs. Conrad nodded her head and crossed her arms over her chest, and began to stare silently out the car window.

And I thought if I'd known blowing my stack was all it took to shut her up, I'd have done it hours ago.

I started the car and we drove into Codderville.

*   *   *

The Family Counseling Clinic was in an old house on Deaver Street, just four blocks from my mother-in-law's. It was a small one-story house, a former two-bedroom. The living room/waiting room had polished pine wood floors covered in bright nylon area rugs. The walls were painted a soft buttery yellow with cream-colored door and window frames. Flower-printed half curtains were on the windows and an ill-assorted grouping of chairs adorned the room. In one corner was a Lego table and other toys.

A young woman, whose rich black hair and beautiful olive complexion bespoke a possible Hispanic heritage, sat at a small desk in the corner by a cold fireplace. Other than the receptionist, we were the only people in the waiting room.

I checked in with the young woman, introducing Brenna. She handed Brenna a clipboard with papers to fill out.

About five minutes later a man came down the hall from one of the bedroom/offices and walked up to us. He was tall, very tall—at least six-six, if not taller. And thin. Very thin. He appeared to be mostly leg; much more than half his height was taken up with those appendages, while his arms hung like ropes at his sides. His size fourteen Reeboks could have housed a homeless family.

He reminded me of a cross between the young Abe Lincoln and Herman Munster. His face was long, his hair dark and in no discernible style; but when he smiled everything changed. He was one of those people—one of the lucky ones—whose smile could literally light up a room. He was wearing an old T-shirt from the 1994 Special Olympics, and faded but creased blue jeans.

He held out a massive, long-fingered hand, and said, "I'm Josh Morgan." I shook his hand, explained who I was, and introduced him to Brenna and Mrs. Conrad.

"I'm just sick about all this here," Mrs. Conrad said, clinging to Josh Morgan's hand. "She's always been such a good girl. And now that the best thing in the world's fixin' to happen—''

"What would that be, Mrs. Conrad?" Morgan asked, his voice calm and concerned.

"Why, my Lorabell's coming home!" She let go of Morgan's hand and pointed to Brenna. "Her mama's finally coming home!"

Brenna and I were standing behind Morgan and Mrs. Conrad. I was probably the only one who saw the girl's skin turn pale and her shoulders quiver.

I spent a quick five minutes in Josh Morgan's office explaining my part in Brenna's dramatic morning. I instinctively liked him. In my years in Houston, working as a volunteer at Crisis Hotline and in other paying jobs I'd had, I'd run into more than my share of mental-health professionals. Not all of them are warm and caring professionals. Some were manipulative, other overpowering. And I'd met more than one whose self-esteem was so low they couldn't possibly help bolster someone else's. Like all professions, the mental-health profession is comprised mostly of human beings. And human beings come in a lot of different flavors of their own mental health.

But Josh Morgan reminded me of Anne Comstock, our family therapist. His concern for this teenager he'd barely met seemed sincere and honest. He listened attentively, without the exaggerated listening techniques employed by too many people these days. No "I'm listening" followed by a professionally sincere frown.

He was a tall, awkward man, but my gut told me he was good at what he did.

After my short time with him he called in both Brenna and her grandmother and I was excused. I told the two women I needed to pick up my kids and I would be back to get them at the end of the hour.

I headed the four blocks to my mother-in-law's, anxious to see my children.

There have been times in my life when I have proclaimed myself to be less than the mother-of-the-year. Actually, as a mother I'd say I sometimes suck big-time. Okay, I often suck big-time.

But I love my kids. I worry about my kids. And one of my biggest worries is what I, as their mother, may be doing to them. Remembering the sight of Brenna on the bridge that morning, I couldn't help but wonder if I was doing any of those things that would cause one of my kids to end up on the wrong side of a bridge railing.

I worry about Bessie. She's not my birth child. We adopted her after her birth family, our best friends, were brutally murdered in the house next door to ours. It was a trauma she may never get over, as much as Willis and I try, and even with the loving professional help of Anne Comstock.

And because I worry so much about Bessie, I have to worry that I'm neglecting Megan and Graham, my birth children.

I worry about strangers, Reye's syndrome, crossing the street, and abusive teachers. I worry about Lyme disease, rusty nails, abandoned wells, seat belts, and whether they're sharing. I worry about the availability of cigarettes, booze, and drugs. I worry about the influence of violence on TV—and in our own backyard.

I worry that Willis and I don't show each other enough affection in front of them—then I worry that we show too much.

Up until that morning, however, the one thing I hadn't worried about was teenage suicide.

Now I was going to put my three kids in the same car with a girl who had just tried to take her own life. Did I try to explain this to them? Or take the chance that they wouldn't ask who this strange girl was riding with them? Or, even worse, take the chance that in all her blathering, Mrs. Conrad wouldn't blurt out all that had happened.

I could call Anne, I told myself. She'd tell me what to do.

Or I could try to be an adult and make this decision on my own.

I picked up the cell phone. Unfortunately, Anne was with a client. I was on my own.

We sat in Vera's living room, the girls on either side of me and Graham sitting on the coffee table in front of me. Vera had kindly stayed in the kitchen, cleaning something.

Graham was antsy. He'd had a play date earlier that day with a friend a block over. He'd had to cancel because of his abusive, neglectful mother. This he told me in no uncertain terms. Sitting on the coffee table and listening to me talk was just adding insult to injury.

"I'm sorry, Graham," I said. "I wouldn't have left you here if it hadn't been important. You understand that, don't you?"

"No," he said.

"I'm sorry."

"Well, sorry doesn't get me over to Taylor's house."

I ate the comeback that sprang to my lips. Somehow, over these long almost ten years, Graham and I have developed an almost equal relationship. We bicker like an old married couple. Anne was trying to reestablish a mother/son relationship. Unfortunately, most of the work was mine, and that included biting back a good rejoinder time after time.

"Something happened I have to tell you about," I said.

Graham rolled his eyes.

I told them what happened that morning, leaving out my diving in the river to save Brenna. That would scare the girls. I just told them that I talked her out of jumping.

"Well, hurrah for you," Graham said. "Can we go now?"

"I want you to know this because we're going to be picking the girl and her grandmother up and taking them home in a few minutes."

"Oh, well great! Now I'm really gonna be late!" my son said.

"You're selfish!" Megan declared, and hit Graham on the arm. I smiled inwardly and didn't scold her. How could I when she did something I'd been dying to do?

"Mama, is she okay?" Bessie asked.

"Yes, honey, she's fine now."

"Why would she *do* that?" Megan asked.

"She was very sad and didn't have anyone to talk to—not like you kids do. Her mom and dad don't live with her."

"Well, that's why then," Bessie said. "She needs a new mom and dad, like I got."

I patted her smooth, dark brown hair. "You're absolutely right, honey. But, since she can't have that, how about some really good friends?"

"Like us?" Megan asked, green eyes big as saucers.

"Yep, like us," I answered.

"Great, a suicidal teenage chick," Graham said. "Is she at least a babe?"

Both girls looked at me. I said, "Get him!"

All three of us grabbed him and got him on the floor, tickling him until he cried uncle.

Although I had asked the kids not to bring up the subject, the first thing Megan said after Brenna and Mrs. Conrad were in the car was "Don't try to kill yourself. I'll be your friend." She patted Brenna on the hand.

Brenna was in the backseat, the girls on either side of her. Graham rode in the cargo area of the station wagon—where there were no seat belts. If I wasn't et up with Southern politeness, I would have stuck Mrs. Conrad back there.

When Megan made her pronouncement, I looked in the rearview and saw Brenna start for a moment. Then she smiled and squeezed Megan's hand. "I'd like that," she said. She turned to Bessie. "Both of you would be good friends."

"Okay," Bessie said. "You like Barbie?"

"Yes, I do," Brenna said.

Bessie nodded. "Okay. You can play with Sweet Dreams Barbie. She's the best."

"No, you can play with my Malibu Barbie. She's better," Megan said.

"No!" Bessie screamed. "I offered first!"

"I talked to her first!" Megan screamed.

"How about if I bring my own Barbie?" Brenna asked.

Both little girls looked at each other for a long moment. Then Megan grinned. "Cool," she said.

"Do you ever read Evil Ernie?" Graham asked Brenna from the cargo area, referring to his favorite nasty, horror comic character.

"Used to. Haven't seen one in a while. What's he up to?"

Graham proceeded to tell her in detail the latest antics of Ernie, in all their gruesome glory.

I smiled to myself. This being responsible for a stranger's life was a piece of cake.

Willis finally spoke to me later that night after the kids were in bed. It had been a long evening. When you're talkative people, a couple who tell each other everything, it's difficult to maintain that icy "I'm not speaking to you until you speak to me" crap. Having three maniacal children two days after Christmas with new toys to destroy helped.

I came back downstairs after having bathed the girls, elicited a promise of a bath in the near future from Graham, my hydrophobic son, and read the girls a chapter in their new Christmas book.

Willis was sitting on the sofa in the living room. Wonder of wonders—the TV wasn't on. Okay, maybe it had something to do with the fact that we were hip deep in Christmastime reruns, but I wanted to think it had more to do with the fact that we needed to talk.

I walked into the living room and sat on the opposite end of the sofa from my husband.

"We have to talk," Willis said.

I nodded my head. "Okay," I said.

"When I met you, the last thing I would have called you was a risk-taker. But I think that's what you're turning into, E.J. When you're nineteen, twenty years old, the risk's not that big. But when you're your age, with three kids, the risk is huge."

"I'm not a risk-taker! Jesus! What does that mean, anyway? I don't jump out of airplanes or climb Mount Everest, for crying out loud—"

"No, but you stick your nose in where it doesn't belong. And every time you do that, *every damn time you do that*, something happens to this family."

I shook my head. "Willis, nothing is going to happen to the family. I helped this girl because I had to. And I know you. And I *know* you would have done the same thing."

Willis sighed. "Why did she do it?"

I shook my head again. "I don't know, yet. I want to find out though." He was frowning. "Willis, she's a good kid. You should have seen her with our kids. They love her."

"She's an emotionally unstable adolescent—"

"Whoa. Listen to you. She's *suicidal*, Willis, not *homicidal*. And something you may not know. I jumped in when she screamed that she couldn't swim. She didn't want to die, honey. She'd been up all night, and whatever demons are around are always a lot bigger when you're suffering from sleep deprivation. Anne says this guy Josh Morgan is really good. As far as I can tell she's been alone for a long time, with nobody but her grandmother for family. And as much as she may love the girl, that woman doesn't have the emotional strength to deal with Brenna right now."

"And you do?" Willis asked, his eyes skeptical.

"*We* do," I said, reaching for his hand. He didn't pull it away. Always a good sign.

Three

As the days dragged closer and closer to the new year, I had an idea. Willis and I are not the "go to a fancy hotel on New Year's Eve and party all night with total strangers" type. For one thing, it costs too damn much. For another, the older we get, the more we find we like being at home. And home is a wonderful place to be on New Year's Eve. You don't have to fight the crowds at clubs and hotels, you don't have to fight the drunks on the freeway; basically, all you have to do is clean up afterward. With three kids, two still young enough to *enjoy* housework, I thought I could get this done.

I decided to throw a party. Not a big one; just us, our neighbor Elena Luna and her two sons, Willis's partner Doug Kingsley and his date of the moment, Willis's secretary, Miss Alice, and her best bud, my mother-in-law Vera. And I thought it would be nice to invite Brenna. Sans grandma.

Earlier I'd finally gotten ahold of Wendy Beck, Monique's best friend, on the phone.

"Oh, Mrs. Pugh, I was just going to call you. I meant to bring the kids some stuff before Christmas, but I ended up going out of town, and I just got back."

"Wendy, you don't have to do that."

"Oh, I know, but I want to. And I want to see Bessie. It's been too long."

We made arrangements for her to come over Monday afternoon, the thirtieth, to see the kids. Wendy was a freshman at Rice University in Houston, and she brought the girls stuffed-owl mascots and Graham a Rice Owls baseball cap that he immediately put on backwards, an affectation I have yet to figure out.

Bessie was shy around her, not having seen Wendy in a while, and it didn't take the kids long to scatter.

"She doesn't really remember me," Wendy said, a sad note in her voice.

"You've grown up, honey." I smiled. "You don't look a lot like the girl who used to hang out next door."

Back then, when Monique had been alive, Wendy was the ugly duckling, hanger-on friend, the shadow beneath the raised wings of popular Monique. She had been a mouse, in every sense of the word. After Monique's death, Wendy had spent a lot of time at our house, wanting to be with Bessie. She'd gained weight and let what little looks she had go.

But then she'd stopped coming by so much, and I'd lost track of her for almost six months. When I saw her again, the ugly duckling had truly turned into a swan. She'd lost the misery fat she'd gained after Monique's death, and had learned to blossom once she was in no one's shadow. Admittedly a lot of it had to do with a new boy who moved to town, but sometimes you take what motivation you can get.

Now, looking at her, I saw another new side of Wendy. Her hair was cut in a sleek new do, making her look even older than her eighteen years. And there was a maturity about her that was visible. College was obviously good for her.

"How's Daniel?" I asked, somehow conjuring up the name of the boy who had started the earlier transformation.

"Oh, we broke up," she said, offhandedly. "He's going to UT, I'm at Rice. It's just too difficult maintaining a long-distance relationship."

"That's true."

"Besides," she said, grinning, reminding me of days long ago, "not all the guys at Rice are nerds. There're some real babes there."

"Yeah?"

"Oh, yeah."

We spent some time going over the various "babish" aspects of Rice men, then I asked, "Do you remember a girl in high school, would have been two years behind you. Her name's Brenna McGraw?"

Wendy frowned in concentration. "A sophomore last year?" I nodded and she shook her head. "I didn't know that many sophomores, Mrs. Pugh. But that name, Brenna . . ." Her face brightened. "Oh, yeah! I think I do know her! From Swamp Creek, right? Dark hair, skinny?"

"That's the one," I said.

"I flunked sophomore biology and had to retake it my senior year. Can you believe it? Gross. Anyway, she was my lab partner for a semester. Weird kid."

"How so?"

Wendy shrugged. "I dunno. Quiet. I can't think of anything in particular, but she just seemed strange. Wore really awful clothes. Seriously out-of-date, but not enough to be retro, you know?"

I nodded.

"Why?" she asked.

I had no intention of breaking Brenna's confidentiality, so I said, somewhat truthfully, "I'm thinking of having her baby-sit."

Wendy shrugged. "Well, I guess that would be okay."

"Wendy, can you think of anything specific?"

She thought for a moment, then her eyes got big. "Oh, jeez. Yeah. A bunch of us were talking one day when we had a substitute. Somebody said something about her mother, and we all started ragging on our moms, and Brenna said . . . Oh, God, what exactly did she say?'' Wendy stopped for a moment, trying to recall the incident. ''One of the girls said she wanted to kill her mom, and Brenna said, 'If you do it, tell me how.' And everybody thought it was just, you know, one of those things you say. But I was looking at Brenna when she said it. And, I swear to you, Mrs. Pugh, she really meant it.''

Teenage girls are the most dramatic creatures on earth. I know this. I used to be a teenage girl. How much of what Wendy remembered could I rely on? That Brenna wore out-of-date clothes I could trust. I'd seen that with my own eyes.

But what teenage girl didn't say, at some time in her life, ''I want to kill my mother''? None that I ever knew. It was a given. If you were a teenager of the female persuasion and you had a mother, you wanted to kill her at least once a week. The other six days you just wanted her to go far, far away.

But Brenna didn't have a mother. Or at least didn't have one living with her. Could she have been making reference to Mrs. Conrad? No one on earth could blame her for that.

But Mrs. Conrad had said at Josh Morgan's office that Brenna's mother was coming home. Was this something that happened often? Did the wayward mom return every few years to make life a little more miserable for the girl?

I remembered the way Brenna had looked when Mrs. Conrad had said those words. ''My Lorabell's coming home. Her mama's finally coming home.''

I tried to put those thoughts aside and get ready for the party the next night. There were toilets that needed cleaning, carpets that needed vacuuming, foods I could prepare ahead of time. I needed to go to the grocery store and the liquor store and the party store. There was so much to do for even an impromptu party like ours.

But the thoughts of Brenna wouldn't go away. Was I

bringing an emotionally disturbed young woman into my home? How much did I really owe this girl just because I saved her life?

And then I remembered the look on her face, when she turned and saw me stopping my car beside her on the bridge. The despair in her eyes, eyes rimmed in red and dripping tears and mascara. The skinny little girl in the pink party dress with the Kleenex hanging out the bodice.

Maybe there's a skinny little girl with a tissue-stuffed bra in all of us, no matter what we were or what we did in high school. We cry out in different ways, most of them not as dramatic as jumping off a bridge. But with tears on a pillow, glass objects thrown across a room, or sex with the wrong boy. We cry out. Maybe Brenna had been crying out for a long time. And no one had heard until I found her on that bridge.

I sighed and told the kids to get their jackets on—we were going to the grocery store.

There was no nice way to get out of inviting Mrs. Conrad to the party. She had to bring Brenna if Brenna was going to come.

Before they arrived, I took my mother-in-law aside. "Would you and Miss Alice keep Mrs. Conrad busy so I can spend some time with Brenna?" I asked.

"She that bad, huh?" Vera asked, raising an eyebrow.

"Well—"

"No problem, E.J. Me and Alice'll sit on her if it comes to that."

Vera wasn't much bigger than Mrs. Conrad, but the thought of Miss Alice, who was almost twice Vera's size, sitting on Mrs. Conrad brought an uncontrollable smile to my lips. "Thanks," I said, happy that I meant it, and happy that after all these years of being married to her son I was finally able to invite my mother-in-law into my house because I wanted to, not because I had to.

When they finally got there, Brenna was wearing a black wool sheath, two sizes too big and ten years too old for her. My girls were anxious to see her and both ran up and hugged her. Even Graham, who I knew would spend most of his time in his room with one or both of Elena Luna's boys, reading nasty comic books, took time off to come up and gravely shake Brenna's hand.

"If you want to later," he said, shrugging nonchalantly, "when you get bored, come on up to my room and I'll show you those comics we talked about."

Brenna smiled. "Sure. I'd like that."

Graham just shrugged again, but I noticed a little more color in his cheeks than usual.

I introduced both Brenna and her grandmother to everyone and was gratified to see the three older women congregate on dining-room chairs next to the table where the food was displayed. With any luck, they'd stay there all night.

I hadn't told my neighbor, Elena Luna, anything about Brenna. Luna is a detective with the Codderville Police Department, and I didn't want her to have any preconceived notions about Brenna.

That may have been a mistake.

Luna's not much of a drinker, but it was New Year's Eve, she only lived next door, which meant no driving, and I guess she was due. She drank a few too many margaritas and began to regale Brenna with stories of the teenagers she'd come across.

After ten minutes of rather amusing but bizarre stories from the Luna files, she said, "Ah, hell, you kids. If you're not offing each other, you're offing yourselves."

The room got totally silent. Half the people in the room, with the exception of Miss Alice, Doug and his date, and, of course, Luna, knew of Brenna's recent history.

I stood up quickly. "Why don't you come in the kitchen and we'll get you some coffee?" I said, grabbing Luna's arm.

"What'd I say?" she asked as I dragged her off the sofa. "Huh? What'd I say?"

Brenna stood up and headed for the downstairs bathroom, where she closed the door quietly behind her.

In the kitchen, after I'd explained how I met Brenna, Luna said, "Well, shit! Why didn't you tell me? Jesus!"

"I didn't want you having any preconceived notions about her—"

"No, better I run off my mouth in front of a roomful of people!" She looked toward the living room. "Where'd she go?"

"She's in the bathroom."

"Let me talk to her," Luna said, heading in that direction.

I grabbed her arm. "Luna, I don't think that's a good idea—"

She stopped and looked at me. She wasn't as drunk as I'd first thought. "Look," she said, "I'm not a total idiot. I work with these kids. I want to apologize. Will you permit me that much?"

I let go of her arm.

The downstairs half bath was tucked under the stairs next to my little closet-office, off the foyer near the kitchen. Luna rapped gently on the door. "Brenna? Mind if I come in a moment?"

The door opened and Luna moved inside.

I went back to the living room, where Willis had gallantly rejuvenated the party chitchat. The only person who made eye contact with me as I entered was Mrs. Conrad—and her eyes were shooting daggers.

We talked Mrs. Conrad into allowing Brenna to spend the night. Graham was more than happy to give up his room to her and sleep in a sleeping bag on the floor of our room.

Whatever had happened between Luna and Brenna in the bathroom must have been positive. The two came out five minutes later laughing. And the party moved on from there.

By midnight, everybody was in a pretty good mood, except Bessie, who didn't like the fact that we woke her up just to ring in the new year. The other two kids, who share my genes, were night owls and we often needed dart guns to get them to bed.

We put on silly hats, blew party horns, sang "Auld Lang Syne" in as many different keys as possible, and toasted with a couple of bottles of champagne. Willis made my evening by pulling me into the kitchen for a more than adequate New Year's Eve kiss.

Doug Kingley's date of the evening, a wanna-be model named Sandra something, had a few more margaritas and a little more champagne than the rest of us. As they were leaving, she hooked an arm over Brenna's shoulder, and said, "Max Factor Professional Lash."

Brenna said, "Huh?"

"You've got terrific skin and great eyes. Don't fuck with your skin, honey, but use what you've got. Those eyes. Enhance them."

"Yes, ma'am," Brenna said.

Sandra let go of her and headed unsteadily for the door. "And don't call me ma'am!" she said. "I'm only twenty-four."

Doug turned at the door and mouthed, "She's thirty-two!" With that, he followed her out to his Miata in the driveway.

Mrs. Conrad was a little harder to get rid of. "I don't mind you staying, Brenna, but you behave yourself." Lowering her voice to a whisper that could only be heard by anyone actually in the house, she said, "And make your bed in the morning! And another thing—"

Vera took hold of her arm. "Millie, me and Alice was thinking of stopping at the Denny's out on the highway for a double chocolate fudge sundae. Wanna come?"

"Well, my hypoglycemia's acting up something fierce. I suppose I could eat."

With that, we were alone; just Willis and me and the kids—and Brenna.

*   *   *

On New Year's Day we took down the Christmas decorations while simultaneously watching football on TV. Brenna came up with a game to occupy the kids in the kitchen: "One hundred and one reasons why I can't wait to get back to school."

"Yuck" was Graham's instant reply.

"Oh, Graham, come on," Brenna pleaded. "It'll be more fun if you play."

I don't think dynamite could have budged Graham at that point.

My son had his first crush; it made me want to cry. I always get a little tearful at my kids' firsts: first tooth, first step, first day of school, first poo-poo in a real toilet.

Maybe you have to be a parent to truly understand.

"Okay," he said, smiling sweetly at Brenna.

"You go first," Brenna said.

"So I can see my friends."

"That's good. Megan?"

"So I can see my teacher!" Megan sang out loud.

"That's what I was gonna say!" Bessie wailed.

"Well, I said it first!" Megan countered.

"You stole it!"

"Girls, girls!" Brenna said, touching each of them. "I think it's great that you both like your teachers so much. Bessie, can you think of another one?"

Bessie crossed her arms over her chest and stuck out her lower lip. "I don't wanna play."

"Okay, then just watch us," Brenna said, turning her back on Bessie.

Damn, I thought. *She's good.* It took months of therapy for me to be able to handle Bessie like that.

Bessie grabbed Brenna's T-shirt. "I got one! I got one!"

Brenna grinned. "Okay, what?"

"Finger paints!"

"That was my next one!" Megan wailed.

"Graham?" Brenna asked, ignoring the rivalry.

"School lunches. I really miss the cafeteria food!"

"Yeah!" both girls chimed in.

With that I left the room. I'd rather watch football than stay there and be insulted.

By midafternoon, the lull had set in. Graham was in his room doing whatever dastardly things he does in there, the girls were in their room with their cats, attempting to dress them in doll clothes, and Willis was asleep in front of the TV.

I boiled some water for tea and Brenna and I sat down at the breakfast-room table with a plate of cookies. I'd loaned her some clothes for the day—a pair of Graham's blue jeans that he was more than willing to have her use, and a T-shirt of mine. The blue jeans fit great—I won't get into how baggy my T-shirt was on her.

The black sheath dress was hanging on a hook on the utility room door. Pouring water over the tea bags, I nodded toward the dress and asked, "Where'd you get it?"

"Huh?" She looked behind her at the dress. "Oh. It's my mother's."

I glanced up. Brenna turned a little red in the face, then said, "When I was fourteen, Grandma decided I'd grown as much as I was going to and told me I could start wearing my mother's clothes. They were just rotting away in the closet. They're a little big for me, but that's okay. Grandma said it would save money."

I suppressed the comment that came immediately to my lips, but there must have been a look on my face. Brenna's face grew a little redder. "Grandma's been supporting me for the last nine years on social security and her government pension, which comes to less than $800 a month."

"I'm sorry," I said. "I didn't mean to be judgmental."

"Nobody really means to be, I suppose," she said, sipping her tea.

"Why don't you keep those—" I started, pointing at the borrowed clothes she was wearing.

Brenna stood up. "Thanks. But we don't take charity." She grabbed the dress off the utility room door and moved into the room, closing the door behind her. When she came out, she was dressed in the black sheath, and the blue jeans and T-shirt were neatly folded and sitting on the washing machine. And I felt like a great big idiot.

I reached for her hand. "Brenna. I'm sorry. I didn't mean to hurt your feel—"

"Of course you didn't. Nobody ever does. The girls giggling when I walk into class don't really *mean* to hurt me. The boys playing tricks on me don't really *mean* to ruin my life!"

I squeezed her hand. The girl tugged at my heart. Mrs. Conrad talked so much it was hard to separate the wheat from the chaff of her monologues. But I did remember, that day in the hospital, her asking Brenna about the party she'd been to the night before. That had never come up again. What party? Did someone at that party hurt her feelings? Say something about the out-of-date pink party dress she was wearing?

"What happened?" I asked.

She pulled her hand away. "Gawd, who died and made you Dear Abby?"

"There's an old Chinese proverb that says when you save someone's life, you become responsible for it," I said, smiling slightly, hoping to make it a joke.

She stood up. "You are not responsible for me. Sometimes, with all the other shit in my life, I think the worst thing that's ever happened to me was you jumping in the water after me!"

She ran out of the kitchen, heading down the foyer to the front door.

I went after her, catching her outside on the driveway. I grabbed her arm and spun her around. "If you want me to drive you home, I will. If you want to come back in the house, that's fine, too. But you *will not* just run away from me."

"You're not my mother!" she said.

"I know I'm not. But who is?" I asked quietly.

That stopped her cold. Taking a deep breath, she said, "No one."

"Come in the house."

She followed me, albeit reluctantly, back into the kitchen. Willis raised his head from the couch as we passed behind him, but I waved for him to go back down. I didn't get an argument.

We sat down to our cooling tea. "What happened that night?" I asked.

She didn't ask what night. With us, there was just one "that night." Brenna shook her head, staring into the teacup.

I touched her hand again. She didn't pull away. "I don't want to be your mother, Brenna. And I know I'm too old to be your friend. How about aunt? Can I be your aunt?"

Her shoulders shook for a moment and I thought she was sobbing, but when she looked up I saw she was laughing. "God, you're a riot," she said.

I wasn't sure if this was a good thing or a bad thing. "And that means?"

She smiled. "Yeah. Be my aunt. I don't have one of those either."

I smiled back. "I have an aunt. My father's much younger sister. I had three sisters of my own, but I was the youngest and we didn't get along well. Aunt Frieda became the person I could really talk to. I'd like to be your Aunt Frieda."

Brenna leaned back in her chair and sipped her tea. Dropping her eyes to the table she said, "There's this boy, Patrick. We're in two classes together, and he'd always ignored me until just before Christmas break."

She looked up at me through her long, dark lashes and I nodded encouragement.

"I always bring my lunch, and I sit outside in the commons and read while I eat. I don't care what the weather's like. The worse the better. Because if the weather's bad, then I can have the entire place to myself." She sighed. "The day we were to leave for Christmas break, Patrick comes up to me while I'm eating. I'm alone out there in the commons, because it was cold and rainy that day. And he sits down and asks me about an English assignment. And we start talking. And he tells me there's going to be a big party at his house the week after Christmas because his parents are going to be in Mexico. And he asks me to come. And I like totally freak.''

She looked at me again, and I nodded. "I always thought he was really cute. Really, really cute.''

I smiled. She didn't.

"So he writes it all down. His address and the time and date. And I say, yeah, great, I'd love to come.''

Brenna took a deep breath. A shudder broke it, almost turning it into a sob. Tears sprang to her eyes. She looked back at the tabletop. "So I got all dressed up and I had Grandma drop me two blocks from Patrick's house because he lives here in Black Cat Ridge, and I didn't want him to see Grandma's car. Or hear it. And I ring the doorbell. Patrick answers and he takes my hand and I go in the living room.'' She sighs. "There are four boys sitting there drinking beer. Nobody else is there at all. And they start hooting and hollering. Telling Patrick he's the greatest. King of 'em all. But this one boy in the corner, he's just sitting there with a beer in his hand, and he says, 'Hell, she's easy. It's always easy to get the geeks.' And Patrick says, 'Bullshit! A bet's a bet! Pay up!' And all the boys start handing him money. Then Patrick looks at me and he grins and it scares me. And he says, 'You ready to party now?' ''

Tears were hitting the top of the table, puddling. I wasn't sure if they were hers or mine, or both.

"I ran for the front door,'' she said. She stopped talking.

I squeezed her hand. "Did they hurt you?'' I asked. I couldn't say the word. Couldn't ask her my real question. Sometimes its hard for a woman's mouth to form the "R'' word.

She was still for over a minute, then she slowly shook her head. "I got outside. The greenbelt's right across the street from Patrick's house. I ran for that." She shook her head. "Really stupid. Like running into the woods, or something."

"They followed you?"

She nodded her head. "They were laughing and hollering and running after me. One of them caught me just inside the greenbelt." She stopped and reached for her cup of tea, taking a large gulp of the now-tepid liquid. "The greenbelt is lighted, you know?"

I nodded my head.

"The one who grabbed me, he . . . he grabbed my dress," she touched her chest, indicating where he had grabbed. "And he pulled it. I guess he was trying to rip my dress off."

I squeezed her hand. It was so inadequate. But it was all I could do.

"I . . . the dress . . . was too big. I . . ."

"Brenna, you don't have to—"

She shook her head, pulling her hand away from mine. "Yeah, I do." She took a deep breath. "The dress was too big and I'd stuffed one of my mom's bras with tissues. That boy . . . he found that. He started laughing. Then they all saw it."

She pulled her hand away. "They didn't rape me, E.J. They were laughing too hard to do that. I started running, and they didn't follow. But now, tomorrow, I have to go back to school. You saved my life and now I have to go back there." She looked at me. "Have I thanked you yet?"

Four

I write romances. Not the great, epic, sweeping sagas, just little category romances. I manage about two a year. It helps with expenses. It's not really what I want to do, what I'd planned on doing.

I wanted to write the great American novel. I was about a quarter of the way through, about three hundred pages, with what I thought was it when I got pregnant with Graham. I put the book aside. A year ago I reread it. I broke a few city ordinances with the bonfire I made of the pages in the backyard.

Someday I'll try again. When I have great gobs of time all in a row. Right now I have the time to churn out a category romance twice a year, and that's what I do.

I try to work it so I finish a book right before Christmas vacation and right before summer vacation. I'd finished the first draft of *On the Sound* the day before the kids got out of classes. Tomorrow, with the start back of school, I'd hoped to get to the second draft.

That wasn't going to happen.

I had a job to do and that was getting Brenna out of Black Cat Ridge High School. Running away, you say? You betcha. I could see no great moral virtue in the girl going back to the shame and humiliation she'd find at the hands of those boys. Boys who, in a fair world, would be locked away from the rest of us.

Brenna would be at their mercy in the halls of Black Cat Ridge High. Their mercy and that of those they told. Because it would get around and get around quickly. Juicy stuff like that always did.

Codderville had its own high school. I would do what I could to get her in there, even if it meant changing her legal address to that of my mother-in-law. It was done all the time. But first I'd try Josh Morgan. If he knew what had happened, he'd help. Maybe.

I tossed and turned all night long, worrying about it. Willis asked me more than once what was wrong, but I couldn't tell him. It was more than betraying a confidence.

I felt, rightly or wrongly, that this was something he could never truly understand. His very maleness excluded him from feeling in his gut what had happened to Brenna. Men don't *feel* rape, and what had happened to the girl was a form of that. Men could try to understand, could get angry for you, could weep for you, but they couldn't *feel* it.

They don't walk to their cars at night with keys splayed in their fingers counting the steps to the car, checking the backseat, doing all those things a woman *must* do. They don't see a form outside their bedroom window at night and know it's a man and know what that man might do.

It's one of those divisions of the sexes that will never heal. Just like I will never know what it feels like to be called "nigger," no man will ever know what the word "rape" makes a woman feel.

Those boys had not entered her body; but they had forced themselves on her against her will, had shamed, humiliated, and degraded her. And they would brag about it.

When I drove Brenna home late that afternoon, I'd told her, "Don't plan on going back to school tomorrow."

She turned and looked at me. "Grandma will make me."

"You need to tell her what—"

"No! Absolutely not," she said.

I nodded my head. "Then be sick. I'm going to find a way to get you moved to Codderville High."

The look she gave me then was the first sign of hope I'd seen on her face. "You think you can?"

"I will," I promised.

I wondered how I would keep that promise.

"I need my tie!" Willis yelled from upstairs.

"Which tie?" I yelled back.

"The one with the carrots on it!"

"Mom, where's my backpack?" Graham asked.

"Mommy, do I put the milk on the cereal or the cereal in the milk?" Megan asked.

"Did you check under your bed?" I asked Graham. "First the cereal and then the milk. In your closet on the same hanger with your navy blazer!" I shouted upstairs.

"Ha! Look at Bessie!" Graham yelled, falling against the wall in ultradramatic laughter.

I looked at Bessie. She had on one Mary Jane and one Junior Ked. "One or the other," I said, grabbing the milk carton out of Megan's hands as she began to splash it liberally across the kitchen table.

"I can't find the other two," Bessie said, sitting on a kitchen chair and dangling her mismatched footwear for the world to see.

"Find your backpack," I told Graham, "and while you're up there, look in the girls' room for a matching shoe."

"Jeez, I have to do *everything*!"

"It's not there!" Willis yelled.

"Then find another tie!"

"But I want that one!"

It was a typical Monday morning in the Pugh household, except that it was Thursday and we'd been off our usual routine for a great deal more than a weekend. Extended periods of time tend to make ties, backpacks, and shoes disappear with abandon.

I was navigating the rocky shores of family life with little more than three hours' sleep, and I was afraid any minute we were going to hit a barrier reef.

"Found it!" Willis said, coming down the stairs two at a time, the carrot tie draped over his arm, and wearing his gray suit.

"Where was it?" I asked, pushing Bessie's chair up to the breakfast table.

He mumbled something.

"I didn't hear that," I said, grabbing the sugar bowl out of Megan's reach as she went for her third teaspoonful.

"On the hanger with the navy blazer," he said. Then he stuck his tongue out at me.

Graham came into the kitchen with his old backpack and one of Megan's shoes—a size larger than Bessie's—that didn't match either the Mary Jane or the Ked.

"Do me," Willis said, sticking his neck out and handing me the carrot tie.

Willis is a blue jeans and work shirt kinda guy. He doesn't do ties. But he had a meeting with a new client that morning, and he was dressin' for impressin'.

I fumbled around, trying for a Windsor knot. It took three tries, but I got it.

"Bessie, finish up quickly and go upstairs and find some matching shoes," I said, snugging the knot to Willis's Adam's apple and straightening his shirt collar.

"They're gone," Bessie said nonchalantly as she splashed her spoon in her bowl, trying to sink the last few Cheerios.

"They are not gone," I said. "They are somewhere in your room. If you don't find them, you will go to school in your stocking feet."

"Okay," she said as she made a bomb noise as the last Cheerio bit the big one.

"Okay what?" I demanded.

"Okay, I'll go to school in my socking feet."

"Stocking feet. No you will not!"

"But you said—"

Willis lifted Bessie up out of the chair, zerberting her tummy in the process. "Upstairs now!" he said. "I want twenty-seven pairs of shoes down here pronto!"

Bessie laughed and ran for the stairs, saying, "Oh, Daddy!" over her shoulder.

He gets giggles and "Oh, Daddy," I thought. *I get nothing but grief.*

I turned to my son. "Where's your new backpack?" I demanded.

"I dunno," he said, pouring milk on his cereal.

"You can't take the old one," I said.

"Sure I can," he said.

"The new one has your schoolbooks in it. It also has the project you worked on for the entire first week of Christmas break!"

"Oh," he said. "Yeah. I forgot."

"Well, where is it?"

He shrugged.

I moved the bowl out of his reach. "Go upstairs and find the *new* backpack!"

"They'll get soggy!" he yelled.

"I don't care!" I yelled back.

He left the room, muttering something under his breath that sounded entirely too much like "ball buster." But I knew my son would never say something like that. Surely.

Mrs. Conrad had a doctor's appointment at eleven that day in Codderville. She'd have to leave fifteen minutes to a half hour before that to make it. I pulled into Brenna's driveway at 11 A.M. on the dot.

As soon as I'd gotten the kids out of the house I'd called and made an emergency appointment with Josh

Morgan. He would see us at eleven-fifteen. Brenna was watching for me and ran out and jumped in the car as I pulled into the driveway.

"Put on your seat belt," I said automatically as I backed out, trying not to look at the print blouse that hung on her like a sack, or the black stretch pants that barely touched her legs.

"You think he can help?" she asked.

"Yes. I definitely think so." I straightened the car out and hightailed it to Codderville. "But you'll have to tell Josh the truth, Brenna. He'll need to know what happened."

She nodded but said nothing as we made our way into town.

When we entered the Family Counseling Clinic, Brenna grabbed my hand and didn't let go. When Josh came out for her, she still held it tight.

"Come with me?" The pleading in her eyes couldn't be ignored.

I looked at Josh, and he nodded.

Once inside, I had to take the lead. Brenna's grip on my hand was enough to stop the blood circulating.

I began, slowly, to tell Josh Morgan what had happened that night, stopping often to give Brenna an opportunity to break in. She didn't.

When I'd finished telling the story as I remembered Brenna telling it, Josh looked at her.

"Brenna, I'm so sorry," he said. He didn't reach for her, or try to touch her. "That must have frightened you badly."

She nodded.

"She can't go back to that school," I said.

Josh nodded. "I agree. Why don't you two wait outside while I make some phone calls?"

His hand was on the phone as we left the office.

Ten minutes later he called us back in.

"Okay, here's the deal," he said, leaning forward, his tall, thin upper body resting on elbows against his knees, talking to Brenna alone. "Do you know Christie Hanson, the counselor at your school?" he asked.

Brenna nodded. "I know who she is, but I've never talked to her."

"She's going to clean out your locker and come by your house late this afternoon to pick up any schoolbooks you have there. Tomorrow, at 8:45, you be in Ms. Reynolds's office at Codderville High. She and Ms. Hanson are talking right now, trying to set your schedule up so you'll be in basically the same two term classes you had at Black Cat. That way you shouldn't lose any credits."

Brenna's mouth was open. So was mine, probably.

"You mean that's it?" Brenna said. "I don't have to go back there?"

"That's it. You're now a Bear instead of a Wildcat."

"Go Bears," I said, smiling at Brenna.

He walked us to the door, Brenna saying thank you over and over.

"Thank me by being back here at, what, four o'clock on Monday? That's your appointment?"

"Yes," she said, smiling up at him.

"Don't miss it," he said, holding the door for us. "Normally, I don't take secondhand stories," he said, glancing deliberately at one then the other of us. "But I understand the emergent nature of the situation. Monday, Brenna, we'll talk about this in detail. Don't miss your appointment."

"I won't," she said. As we started down the hall, Brenna turned, and said, "Thank you."

Josh was still standing at the door to his office, watching us. That "light up a room" smile played across his lips. "You're welcome," he said.

We went outside to the car.

"I can't believe it!" Brenna said. She turned and hugged me.

"Don't thank me," I said, hugging her back. "Josh did it."

"Yeah, but you made him."

I started the car and pulled onto the street. "Look, we have a few more minutes before I need to get you back," I said. "I'd like to buy you a Christmas present."

"No way! I need to buy you one!"

"Do you have any money?"

Brenna looked crestfallen. "No," she said.

"Then I'll buy us both one!" I grinned and, in a minute she followed suit.

I took her to the boutique in the mall where Wendy Beck used to work. I remembered thinking how great the clothes were when I'd gone to see Wendy there. There wasn't a thing in the store I could wear—they didn't go up to my size, nor did they cater to the middle-aged house-wife and mother look I wear so well.

We found Brenna a pair of designer jeans that fit like a glove, a form-fitting lace bodysuit, and a little denim jacket. She was transformed. I found it amazing to see the nice body that had been hidden under her mother's eighties rejects. Because of boutique prices, the three little items cost a bundle, but it was worth it to see the look on her face.

Although I never played with dolls much as a child, when my children were first born I found myself playing dress up with them—especially Megan, my beautiful pale-skinned, strawberry blond doll. When we inherited Bessie when both girls were four, I had a great time dressing them in matching outfits (although I was careful to pick different colors to give them each a sense of individual-ity—I'd read that somewhere).

Shortly after entering the first grade, my daughter Megan began screaming in the mornings when I picked out her clothes. Bessie, on the other hand, being quieter and sneakier, just laid out her clothes the night before and would brook no argument from me in the morning.

I'll never forget the morning I came in their room and Bessie was efficiently pulling on pink-and-white-striped pants to go with the orange blouse with green pockets.

"Bessie, honey, you can't wear that," I'd said.

"Why not?" she reasoned. "It's very cool."

You can't argue fashion sense with a six-year-old.

Which is one of the reasons I was having such a great time shopping with Brenna—she actually wanted my opinion. I had a teenage doll—my very own Barbie—to dress.

We left the mall, with me wondering what she'd wear on day two of her new life as a Codderville High Bear. That's when I wheeled the car into the Wal-Mart parking lot and dragged her inside.

For the same price I'd paid for the three items at the boutique, I got her a second pair of jeans, these black and snug, a denim miniskirt, a red turtleneck, two way-cool T-shirts, a pair of black tights, two bras that fit, a packet of three bikini underpants, one more expensive pair of panties—lacy bikinis—a down jacket, and a sweater dress that hugged her in all the right spots.

"Mix and match," I told her, "and you'll have enough to last you till spring and beyond."

"Like what with what?"

We planned her wardrobe as we loaded the car with our packages. Driving back to Brenna's house, I rehearsed in my head all the explanations and excuses I'd need when Willis saw the Visa bill.

Pulling into Brenna's driveway, I knew the fun part was now over. It was time to convince Brenna that her grandmother had to be told something.

"Your grandmother has to know," I said. "She'll have to drive you to school. You won't get bus service to Codderville."

Brenna nodded as she opened the door. "Maybe we could—" she started, but the front door opened and Millie Conrad, cigarette in hand, came running toward the car.

"Where have you been!" she screeched. "I thought you done run off! You scared the liver out of me, girl!"

"Hey, Grandma, I'm sorry—"

"Hey, Nurse E.J., how you?"

"I'm fine, Mrs.—"

"Lordy, Brenna, the most wonderful thing's happened—"

The front door of the little doll-like house opened again and a woman walked down the two steps. She was about my age, maybe a little older, taller than both Mrs. Conrad and Brenna, maybe five-seven, and somewhat overweight. Her hair was shoulder length and badly permed, white-blond with about an inch of dark root showing.

Brenna was standing by my side, and I felt her stiffen at the sight of the woman walking toward us. I looked at the girl. Her face had gone ashen and her hands were trembling.

"Lookee who's here! My Lorabell's come home early!" Mrs. Conrad shouted, grabbing her daughter by the arm. "Lookee, Lorabell, here's your little girl all growed up!"

Lorabell looked at Brenna and nodded. There was no emotion on the woman's face. "Hi," she said. "How you doing?"

Brenna didn't respond. The color that had fled her face rushed back, bringing with it a dull redness that covered her from the neck up.

"And this here is the nurse lady I been telling you about, Lorabell," Mrs. Conrad said. "Nurse E.J."

I held out my hand to Brenna's mother. Lorabell looked at it for a full ten seconds before extending her own. We shook briefly. Her hand was rough, work-worn, with calluses and broken nails.

Up close I could see she wore makeup, but even that couldn't hide the ravaged skin. Pockmarks marred the cheeks, and dark circles bagged the eyes.

"Hi, I'm Lori Tyler," she said.

I may have made a sound. Of surprise, shock. Revulsion.

I usually have a fairly good poker face, but this was something I never suspected.

Lori Tyler. Brenna's mother was Lori Tyler. I wouldn't have recognized her without the name.

I turned to Brenna and saw her looking at me. Trying to cover, I said, "We need to speak with your grandmother—"

"I'll take care of it, E.J. Thanks." Her voice was cold. She started to walk toward the house.

"Brenna, the stuff in the car—"

"Later," she said, not looking back.

I nodded at Mrs. Conrad and her daughter and, saying something inane, like, "See ya," got in the car and headed back to Black Cat Ridge, as fast as the station wagon would let me.

Stories like Lori Tyler's happen all the time. They're on the news, in the papers, magazines, so much so that you get a little immune to them. But Lori's story had happened in my own backyard, so to speak. We were living in Houston at the time. The incident happened in Cypress-Fairbanks, a suburb outside Houston.

Even then I might not have paid all that much attention to it, except that I was very pregnant with Graham at the time. "The bunny died" might not have been music to my ears, but by my eighth month I was pretty much into the whole scene. And hormones were running rampant throughout my body.

I became obsessed with the story. Followed it on the six o'clock news every evening, even started taking the daily paper so I could follow it in all the gory details. I had plans to attend the trial, but Willis found out and we had one of our little *talks*. I didn't go to the trial.

By my calculations, Lorabell Conrad McGraw Tyler had served only nine years of the life sentence she received from the state of Texas.

But I think it's safe to say I knew as much about what went on, and the history behind it, as anyone who wasn't personally involved.

Lori, as her friends called her, had had a run of bad luck, mostly with men.

She married Larry McGraw at age seventeen and gave

birth to a little girl, who I now knew was Brenna, shortly after the ceremony. McGraw was a doper and a drinker and used Lori as a punching bag. When she got pregnant with her second child, she took three-year-old Brenna and left.

She moved in with her mother and gave birth to a son, whom she named Branson Lee. According to all reports, he was a sickly baby, fussy and out of sorts most of the time. Lori met and moved in with David Tyler when the baby was no more than six months old. Brenna had just turned four.

After her divorce from Larry McGraw, Lori married David Tyler. David was a good man, according to neighbors, family, and witnesses at the trial. He had a decent job and worked hard. He didn't drink, and he didn't do dope. And he didn't beat Lori.

He was, however, a strict disciplinarian with the children. Brenna had to recite her alphabet or do sums before she could eat dinner. David didn't believe in children missing school, and when, in the first grade, Brenna was sent home from school with a fever, David took off work, went to the house, took her out of bed, made Lori put her clothes back on her, and walked her the five blocks to the school. When the school refused to receive the child with a high fever, David withdrew her from attendance that very day. Brenna got home schooling from that point on.

Brenna was six and Branson two when they began home schooling. David's theory was that a child was never too young to learn. Branson was still a sickly child. He had allergies and caught cold a lot.

David didn't believe in allergies. He thought Lori coddled Branson too much. He forced the little boy to eat bread, even though the doctor said he was allergic to wheat. Forced him to drink milk, although the child was lactose intolerant and got severe diarrhea from any milk product.

David said he would grow out of this ''silliness'' if his body could just get used to the foods he was supposedly allergic to. Instead, Branson just stayed sick most of the time.

David began to show disdain for his wife's youngest child. David didn't like sickness; people who were sick all the time were really just weak, according to David. To strengthen Branson he would leave him outside all day in the cold and rain—to let his body acclimate. When the baby would cry he would put him in a closet—to toughen him and "help" with the boy's fear of the dark.

He spanked him and shook him and slapped him.

But all for the boy's own good. David rarely lost his temper. He never laid a hand on either child out of anger.

When Brenna was seven years old and Branson three, she was working her multiplication tables and he was supposed to be adding up sums of three. Branson couldn't do it.

As the evening wore on and Branson still couldn't add up sums of three, even after David spanked him, even after David slapped his face, even after David threatened him with the closet, David came up with something new.

It was August in Houston, Texas, the equivalent of hell. The house had window units, one in the living room and one in the master bedroom. The children's rooms were not air-conditioned.

At nine o'clock, in front of Lori and Brenna, he wrapped the baby up in a blanket, taped the blanket with duct tape, and laid the boy on his bed in the un–air-conditioned room.

"I'll sweat the stupid out of you," David said, calmly, as he shut the door and left the boy, wrapped in the blanket, in the ninety-plus-degree room. David had decided that Branson could stay that way until morning.

Lori claimed at trial that she'd told David she didn't think it was such a good idea. But a look from David shut her up. Brenna said nothing. She went on with her home schooling, classes that lasted from seven in the morning until ten at night six days a week, and from after church until ten on Sundays. She was getting pretty good at the multiplication table, and was proud that she was learning something most kids didn't learn until they were much older.

At six the next morning, Lori used scissors to cut the duct tape holding the blanket around her son. As she unwrapped him from his cocoon, she found him limp and unresponsive. Concerned, she and David rushed the boy to the hospital.

He died two days later.

At first they told authorities that Branson must have gotten trapped in his blankets and they didn't hear him yelling for help. But the police questioned the boy's older sister, Brenna, and she told of Daddy's new method to help Branson learn.

Lori was next to break down. She told the authorities what had happened. David never confessed.

The couple turned against each other, each blaming the other for the baby's death.

But witnesses, friends and relatives, told authorities of David's methods, David's idea of discipline. And of Lori's compliance.

They had separate attorneys, separate trials. Both received life imprisonment. Six months later, David Tyler was back in front of a judge. His lawyer had appealed the case on a technicality. A little more than a year after Branson Lee McGraw had been laid to rest, David Tyler was walking the streets, a free man.

Lori served her time. Not all of it, of course. No one ever does.

My stomach ached at the thought of what Brenna had gone through. The horror that had been her early life, the guilt she must bear as witness. By the time I got in my house, I barely made it to the downstairs bathroom before I lost my breakfast.

All I could see, as I retched into the toilet, was the look on Brenna's face when she saw that I knew her secret. And that the secret repulsed me.

Five

The new year brought with it our first real cold snap. We had a hard freeze one night that necessitated the covering of delicate plants and shrubs, and bringing in the cats from their usual nocturnal adventures.

Megan could only find one of her wool mittens, and Graham had no idea where his heavy coat might be.

Willis spent most of that evening before the hard freeze outside with torn-up rags and duct tape wrapping exposed pipes. This necessitated a lot of money into the cussing jar—witnessed and attested to by his helpers Bessie and Megan—and the destruction of a brand-new sheet mistaken—supposedly—for a rag.

In the front yard I heard Bob Mitchell, our neighbor newly down from Detroit, laughing at Willis's antics. "Better get out the snow tires, Willis, they say it could get down to thirty-two!"

Brenna wouldn't speak to me, and I spent a lot of time thinking of her and worrying about her. My newfound information shed a whole new light on the incident at the bridge.

This was a child with a horrendous past and a nebulous future. The mother who had condoned and abetted Brenna's early abuse, the mother who had allowed Brenna's only sibling to die at the hands of David Tyler, was coming home. To have a weight like that hanging over her, and then to have been treated so shabbily by the boys at Black Cat Ridge High—it's a wonder she had cried for help at all as she was being washed downstream.

But there is something very strong about the human will to live. That spark that can last so long. I remembered my great-grandmother, who held on to life so desperately, even thought she was blind and deaf and unable to remember her loved ones. She was ninety-eight and had spent four years in that condition before the spark finally died out, finally allowed her to go.

Is there something in human nature that tells us that just around that corner, just around that bend, something better is coming? We can make it if we just hold on?

There are those who don't have it, or had that spark extinguished at such an early age they never knew it existed. Children who see their friends and family members killed one after the other until life has little meaning, who join gangs and kill and maim at tender ages because they never felt that spark, never knew it was there.

Brenna could have been one of those kids. But somewhere the spark burned; maybe just a flicker, but it was enough for her to call out—enough for her to know that there could be something out there. Something not so bad as what had come before.

I hoped I hadn't been that something. I hoped she hadn't been banking on me to be the one to pull her through, because I had disappointed her mightily. When she needed my strength to back her up, she'd been met by my revulsion at who her mother was. I had to get us both beyond that, but it would be hard to do if she refused to speak to me.

I called the house every day and got endless recitations from Mrs. Conrad on what Lorabell was up to and what an ungrateful little brat Brenna was, and massive apologies that the girl wouldn't come to the phone.

I'd planned on taking her that Monday to her appointment with Josh Morgan, but Mrs. Conrad said she'd do it, and the sound of her voice let me know she was doing it grudgingly.

Every phone call got me a litany of complaints from Mrs. Conrad.

"Why, that girl hardly speaks to her own mama! Can you believe it?

"My back is just acting up something awful with all this driving I'm having to do! Taking that girl all the way into Codderville to go to high school! I ask you! Why in the world can't she be satisfied with a fine school like Black Cat Ridge? I mean, I can't believe that little old Codderville school's got better courses than that spankin'-new Black Cat Ridge school!

"Now I'm having to pick her up at the blasted school and drive her over to that crazy doctor's place ever day! Why does she have to see him ever day? Why does she have to see him at all? I think this is all just silliness!"

And on and on and on.

On the fifth day, I picked up my children from school, using them as bait, I am not proud to admit, and drove to Brenna's house. She and Mrs. Conrad were just pulling in the driveway when we got there.

The cold front had broken and the sun was shining brightly. It was still coat weather, but the temperature was in the mid-fifties and livable, even for us warm-blooded central Texans.

Bessie and Megan bailed out of the car, running up to Brenna for a hug. Graham was more nonchalant, although obviously as eager to see her. I grabbed all the goodies Brenna and I had bought the week before out of the back of the station wagon and walked with them up the sidewalk to the house.

"I've been meaning to get these to you," I said, handing them to Brenna.

She could do nothing but take them.

"Oh, goodness, what's all this?" Mrs. Conrad said, trying to peek in the sacks.

"My Christmas present to Brenna. Some new clothes for her new school."

"Why, Nurse E.J., isn't that just the sweetest thing! You are just the angel I knew you were all along!"

The door opened behind Brenna and Lori Tyler looked out. "Whatja got?" she asked Brenna.

Brenna moved beyond her into the house, ignoring her mother and speaking instead to my children. "Y'all wanna see my room?"

The chorus of yesses could have bowled over weaker individuals.

"Now, Nurse E.J., you just come on in this house!" Mrs. Conrad said.

Lori nodded at me as I moved inside. I said hello.

The front door opened directly into the living room. There was a tiny faux fireplace in the tiny living room/dining room combo, and I could see an even smaller kitchen at the back of the house. A short hall to the right of the living room must have led to no more than two bedrooms. A pile of linens—blankets and pillows and sheets—next to the sofa, was evidence of where someone—Lori, I hoped—was sleeping.

I found it difficult to look at Lori Tyler. I know, I know, I keep saying what a great big old liberal I am. I'm supposed to believe in rehabilitation and the goodness of the human spirit and all that crap. Excuse me. This woman stood by while a man systematically beat, abused, and killed her child. I won't go so far as to say I found her guiltier than David Tyler—but I did find her *as* guilty. She might never have laid a hand on either of her children, but she stood by and watched while someone else did.

In a fair world, Branson Lee McGraw would be twelve years old now. In the sixth or seventh grade. He might have outgrown his allergies by this time, might have been into sports, or stamp collecting, or just sneaking dirty magazines into his bedroom to hide under the mattress. But he would be alive to become whatever kind of person he chose to become.

Lori Tyler hadn't allowed that to happen. And in doing so had stunted her surviving daughter, leaving her weak and without defenses.

I didn't like Lori Tyler. And I didn't wish her well.

And I didn't want to be sitting in the living room having tea with Lori Tyler and her mother. I wanted to be back in the bedroom, playing Barbies with Brenna and my kids.

But I did have tea. Iced tea. With too much sugar and a sprig of mint. I don't like mint in my tea, but as it came to me that way, I didn't seem to have an option. But then, at that point, I would have found fault with anything either of these women did.

The one good thing about Mrs. Conrad was that I didn't have to try to keep up my end of any conversation. There wasn't any conversation. Just the usual diatribe monologue delivered by Brenna's grandmother.

I tuned out most of it, not caring what she had to say. But something sneaked its way in.

"Did Brenna tell you my Lorabell's getting married again?" Mrs. Conrad said, beaming at her daughter.

"Not getting married again, Ma," Lori interrupted. "Just renewing our vows."

I looked at her. I could feel the blood pumping in my veins. Could feel a vein vibrating at my neck.

"Well, David and her never did get a divorce," Mrs. Conrad said, "and now they're getting back together."

Lori looked at me. Defiantly. "Brenna's daddy and I have been seeing each other some. He used to come up to the prison on visiting days. He always said how unfair it was that I had to be in there."

"David Tyler is not Brenna's father," I said. Maybe too loudly.

"He's the only father she ever knew," Lori said.

"And that's a damned crying shame," I said, standing up. "If you'll excuse me, I want to speak to Brenna a minute."

Lori stood up, too. "It was real nice you helping out Brenna and all, but she won't be needing your help any longer. When David and me renew our vows, Brenna and I will be moving back to Houston with him."

I turned toward the doorway that led to the hall. Brenna and my daughters were standing there.

"Oh, no!" Megan said, grabbing Brenna's hand. "You're moving?"

"Not if I can help it," Brenna said, staring at her mother.

I moved into the hallway. "Brenna, may I speak with you?"

I found her room and moved the kids and Barbies out into the hallway. "Graham, watch your sisters," I said.

"Why? They gonna do tricks?" he asked, glancing at Brenna to make sure she saw how clever he was.

I shut the door and leaned against it.

Brenna was sitting on the bed. It was a small room, with only a twin bed covered with an old quilt, too beat-up to be of any antique value, a plywood chest of drawers, and a wavy, dime-store mirror hanging on the wall. She had spiced the walls up with pictures pulled from magazines—of rock stars, supermodels, and several of Keanu Reeves in various movie roles.

"Brenna, I'm sorry—" I started.

She shook her head. "Why? Why are you sorry? What did you do? Get a little sick to your stomach when you figured out who my mother is? No big deal. You didn't vomit on my shoes E.J. That's better than most people do when they find out what great stock I come from."

I sat down on the bed next to her. "You know," I said, "you might turn into a pretty good kid one of these days. If you ever stop feeling so damned sorry for yourself."

Brenna jumped up and glared at me. "Hey! My life's crap! Or haven't you noticed?"

"You have been through some major shit, I'll give you that. But your life is what you make of it, Brenna. Not what other people do to it."

"Did my loving grandmother mention that she's pulling me out of Codderville High? She says I can just go to Black Cat until we move to Houston." She looked at me defiantly. "Well, I'm not going to Houston! Not now—not ever! I'll kill the bitch before I let her take me back to him!"

We were getting ready for bed. It had been a long night. My mind was so full of Brenna's problems, I didn't have much room for anything else. Supper had been the quick one: macaroni and cheese with cut-up hot dogs. I don't usually serve that when Willis is home. It's a special treat for the kids for those nights when Daddy's working late.

I'm not sure if it was my own distraction or dinner, but Willis and I didn't talk much. Come to think of it, Willis and I hadn't been talking much at all lately. I got the distinct impression he didn't approve of Brenna; and he probably got the distinct impression that I really didn't give a damn about his approval. Don't try to look this up in the marriage manual on "How to Make a Marriage Work." It's not there.

I was in the bathroom, door opened into the bedroom, trying out a new moisturizer my mother had recommended, when my eyes focused in the mirror on the bedroom behind me. Willis was sitting on the side of the bed, wearing only his shorts, staring at me. Our eyes met. It could easily have been the prelude to an interesting evening, but then he looked away, picking up a magazine off his nightstand and lying down on the bed.

I finished rubbing the new crap on my face and went into the bedroom.

"Willis?"

"Um?" He didn't take his eyes off the magazine, although I doubted seriously he was actually reading it. It wasn't *Rolling Stone* or even *Popular Mechanics;* what he had in his hands was a copy of *Jack and Jill,* discarded earlier when I caught the girls in my room trying on my makeup.

"Are we having a problem?" I asked.

He threw the magazine on the floor and looked at me. "Probably," he said.

I made a motion to sit on his side of the bed, so he pulled his feet up. I sat down, resting one arm on his upraised knees.

"I love you," I said.

He smiled slightly. "Always nice to hear," he said.

"But?" I asked.

He sighed and leaned his head back against the pillows. "I feel like a total shit," he said.

"Why?" I asked, making circles with my index finger on his knee.

"It's pretty rotten to be jealous of a sixteen-year-old girl with suicidal tendencies," he said, still not looking at me.

"She's so needy, honey," I said.

"So am I," he said.

Oh boy, I thought. I had a topic I wanted to broach, but I wasn't sure now was the time. The problem was, time was of the essence, and it was basically now or never.

There was so much Willis didn't know, because there was so much I hadn't told him. I started at the beginning, telling him about the night of the "party" and the boys from Black Cat Ridge High School.

By the time I'd finished he was sitting up in bed, his arms around me. "Why didn't you tell me?" he said. Then he shook his head. "That's not important. I think I know. Baby, do you have any idea what I go through in a given week? Have I ever told you about getting into an elevator with a woman alone and feeling her fear? I do, babe, believe me. It happened the other day when I went for that bid. An older woman. I got on the elevator and she was already there and she moved as far as she could to the front corner so she could be by the emergency button, just in case I was a maniac of some sort." He sighed. "I don't blame her, honey. I really don't. But I got in there and stood as far away from her as possible and just stood stock-still. I didn't want to make any move that would make her nervous."

"Willis—"

"It happens all the time. In parking lots. If I see a woman in any underground parking lot, I'll stay as far away from her as possible. I'll walk out of my way to stay out of hers. Shit, I was at the store the other day and saw a teenage girl getting out of a car with a seriously low tire. A couple of years ago, I would have told her to get the damned tire fixed. But not anymore. Instead of taking the chance of scaring her or looking like some pervert to a passerby, I set it up for the poor kid to have a flat tire out on some lonely road where she might end up with a real serial killer!"

He pushed the covers aside and got out of bed, pacing the carpet. "You didn't think I could understand what happened to her."

"On a gut level, honey, you can't."

"Bullshit," he said. "Bullshit. You know what my gut did when you told me what happened to her? It heaved! I felt like vomiting! Is that how you felt?"

I nodded my head.

"So how's that different?" he demanded.

I reached for his hands, pulling him toward me. "It's not, I guess," I said. I looked up into those big brown eyes. "I'm sorry," I said. "I guess I was being overly sensitive."

"Or maybe you just wanted to keep all of Brenna's problems to yourself," he said. "Maybe you didn't want to share her with me."

I let go of his hands and headed toward the bathroom. "Now that's a little sick, don't you think?" I said.

He grabbed my arm. "No, babe. Not sick. Human nature. You saved the girl's life. She's yours. If you tell me all that's going on, maybe I would want to help. Then she's ours. Not just yours."

I rested my head against the doorjamb, wondering if there was a grain of truth in what Willis said.

Willis was a fixer; a male trait my husband possessed in abundance. I could never just bitch to him about something. He always wanted to *fix* it. But with Brenna, I'd been the fixer. I was the one accomplishing, or trying to accomplish, the girl's salvation.

I'd gotten her out of Black Cat Ridge and into Codderville High—with the help of Josh Morgan.

I'd gotten her out of her mother's outdated clothes and into some truly righteous duds.

I was half-afraid to tell Willis what I'd accomplished— afraid he'd think it wasn't enough, afraid he'd try to *fix it better.*

Finally, I sat down on the side of the bed and told him what I'd accomplished—moving Brenna from one high school to the other.

"Damn," he said, smiling, "that's good. I probably wouldn't have thought of that."

I rolled my eyes. "Don't patronize me, Willis. I mean it!"

He looked indignant. "I'm not! My solution to the problem would be to go over to that kid's house and beat the crap out of him."

I smiled at him. "A very manly answer, honey."

"Actually, I still think it's not a half-bad idea."

So then I took a deep breath and told him about the clothes I'd charged to our Visa bill.

Willis frowned. "You know, I noticed the kid did kinda dress funny." Then, of course, he had to revert to "husband" Willis and ask, "How much altogether?"

He tried to stifle his cringe when I told him.

"You remember when I was pregnant with Graham?"

"How could I possibly forget the most terrifying nine months of my life?" he asked.

"Remember the David and Lori Tyler trial?"

He shook his head. I reminded him, telling the story as briefly as possible.

"Okay, yeah, I remember that. What about it?"

"Brenna is the Tylers' surviving child."

"Jesus Christ."

"And Lori just got out of prison, and she's getting back together with David Tyler. And she wants to take Brenna with her."

Willis jumped up and began pacing the bedroom floor. "This is the biggest piece of crap I've ever heard!" he said.

"Yep. Now, here's a partial solution to the problem," I said. He looked at me. "I want to buy a new car."

We really couldn't afford a brand-new car; of course, neither would a brand-new car totally break us. We didn't have a car note; my station wagon was ten years old and paid for. Willis's Karmann Ghia, although now a classic, was bought by him when it was basically just a used car, and had been paid for with cash.

A new car would mean not going on family outings for a while, maybe macaroni and cheese without the hot dogs, and I'd get to wear the same swimsuit I'd been wearing for the last six years.

Or, Willis suggested, we could buy a new *used* car and at least get to have hot dogs with the macaroni and cheese. But whatever we did, we had to do it quickly.

Brenna was sixteen and therefore eligible for driver's ed and a driver's license. I wasn't sure if she'd taken driver's ed yet, but we'd figure something out. I planned on giving her the old station wagon.

This didn't alleviate the problem of moving to Houston, but it meant she could at least stay at Codderville High until Willis and I figured a way for her not to go. And, when she had the license and her own car, it would give her some independence.

The next day was Saturday, and I called Brenna to tell her the plan.

"You can't give me a car!" she whispered. "That's crazy!"

"No it's not," I said. "Brenna, you've seen it. It's an old car. It's five different colors. It's not like we're talking a new Porsche or something."

"I don't have a driver's license, and I'm not signed up for driver's ed—" she started.

"There's a private driving school over at the mall. I already called them and signed you up. You start immediately in an accelerated program, and we can get you a hardship license right away."

There was silence on her end of the phone.

"Honey," I said, "this is a done deal. I've already paid for the lessons and made arrangements for the license."

"Gawd, E.J.—" I could hear her start to cry.

"If you wanna cry about it, fine, Brenna. But there's no need. This will keep you at Codderville High. And keep you going to Josh Morgan's office."

"But Lorabell keeps talking about Houston—"

"Have you heard from or seen David yet?" I asked, my stomach clenching at the mere mention of his name.

"No. But I hear her sometimes on the phone after I'm in bed. I'm pretty sure she's talking to him."

"Have they set a date?"

"Not that they've told me about," she said. "Of course, it's not like Lorabell and I have any long, soul-searching conversations around here."

"You okay?" I asked.

She sighed. "It's kinda rough," she said. "Grandma's bitching at me all the time when I'm outta my room, so I just don't get outta my room much."

"I'm sorry, honey," I said.

"Why are you apologizing—"

I laughed. "Brenna, I'm not apologizing. I'm just sorry you're going through such hell. I wish I could do more—"

"A car! Jeez, E.J. A car!"

I laughed again. "Yeah. A ten-year-old piece-of-junk

station wagon. But it runs. And it should last you a year or two.''

"My own car," she said, her voice quiet.

"The pink slip will be in your name," I said.

"I can get a job," she said. "An after-school job. That would pay for the insurance, right?''

Good thinking, I thought, not having considered the problem of insurance myself. "Yeah. We'll work something out on that. An after-school job's probably a good idea.''

"Thanks, E.J.," she said.

"How are your new clothes?" I asked.

"Ooo, I wore that sweater dress with a pair of boots I found in Lorabell's closet . . .''

We found a four-year-old minivan in a condition and price range we could afford at the used-car lot of the local Ford dealership. The Ford dealership is in downtown Codderville, which consists of two blocks of retail and the county courthouse. Immediately across the street from the dealership is the Burger Hut, the best place in the world to get hamburgers that drip grease right down your arm and french fries so greasy they shine.

I was trying to convince Willis that his cholesterol count would not warrant a trip to the Burger Hut when the door to said establishment opened and a woman walked out. It took me a minute to recognize her. She was dressed up, in a miniskirt and silky blouse, and her hair had been done. The only time I'd seen her had been in grubbies with an inch of black root.

But it was definitely Lori Tyler.

A man came out immediately behind her. Lori turned toward the parking lot of the Burger Hut, but the man grabbed her arm. From across the street, I couldn't hear their words, but the tone of voice was evident. His was pleading, hers angry.

Lori jerked her arm away and stormed to the car in the parking lot. If I'd had any doubt it was Lori Tyler, those

doubts were relieved when I saw the car she got into—
Millie Conrad's 1972 Ford LTD.

The man stood there, looking after her. He was tall, at
least Willis's height, six-foot-two, maybe taller; or maybe
he just looked that way because he was so thin. He had
one of those protruding bellies skinny men get as they
age, thin hair, brown turning gray, and a very protruding
Adam's apple.

He stood there for a moment, then turned abruptly and
walked away, the opposite direction of the parking lot.

As Lori started up the LTD and escaped the parking
lot, Willis said, "What are you staring at?"

"That woman in the old Ford—that's Lori Tyler," I
said.

"Where?"

I nodded in the direction the Ford was moving.

"The blond in the miniskirt who came out of the Burger
Hut?" he asked.

I punched my husband lightly in the ribs. "I'm so glad
you didn't notice," I said.

"Notice what?" he asked in feigned innocence.

"You actually think she's good-looking?"

Willis shrugged as we moved toward the old station
wagon. "In a used-up, disgusting, sexy sort of way."

I let that one lie.

It took us two days to get the minivan—they had to
clean it and fix a few things before we took possession.
In the meantime, Brenna got her learner's permit and
began driver's ed class. Once we got the minivan, we gave
her the station wagon for school.

There was no more mention of Houston. Whatever Lorabell's plans, she was keeping them to herself, but Brenna
was losing weight from the anxiety of it.

On the Friday of that week, after waiting in the living
room/waiting room of the Family Counseling Clinic with
three bored kids, I asked Josh Morgan when he walked
Brenna out if I could speak with him for just a moment.

He graciously took me back to his room while Brenna stayed with the kids.

"I'm really worried about Lori's proposed move to Houston," I told Josh.

His "light up a room" smile wasn't present today. "So am I," he said.

"What can be done to stop this?" I asked.

He shook his head. "I've already talked to a friend in the state child-welfare system. She says that there's nothing the state can do—or, more to the point, would be willing to do. Lori did her time. David, for whatever horrible reason, was released. There's no reason the state can take Brenna away from them."

"Josh, I don't know what to do. I'm at my wit's end. That kid can't end up in the same house with David Tyler again!" I said.

He rubbed his long face with both hands. "She shouldn't even be in the same house with her mother." He shook his head. "E.J., I wish I had some good news for you on this point, but I don't."

He stood up, and I followed, moving to the door. "Maybe we can think of something if we put our heads together," I said.

He smiled, a ghost of his usual smile. "Maybe," he said.

The phone rang at midnight. Willis can sleep through anything, which makes the fact that the phone is on his side of the bed patently absurd, but there you go. I leaned over him and picked up the receiver.

"Hello?"

"E.J.!"

"Brenna?"

"E.J., I just heard them talking—"

"Who, honey?"

"Lorabell and Grandma. The bitch just told Grandma that we're moving next week! Next week, E.J.! God, what am I gonna do?"

I pulled the cord over Willis's prone body and lay back in the bed. "Oh, honey, we'll think of something," I said.

"I'm running away!"

"No, Brenna, you can't do that."

"Why not? It's the best solution! It's the only solution!"

"We'll talk to Josh—"

"I already tried that! I called him first—"

"At this time of night?"

"He gave me his home number for emergencies. But he wasn't there. I just left a message. But he's not going to do any good! What can he do? What can anybody do?" she sobbed.

I talked to her for over an hour, trying to soothe her, trying to convince her not to run away. She agreed by the end of the call to wait until the weekend before she made any decision. Unfortunately, the decision was made for everyone way before the weekend.

The phone rang while I was standing in the kitchen contemplating taking a nap. It had been a long night. Although talking to Brenna on the phone had only kept me up till a little after one, the tossing and turning and worrying kept me up a lot longer. And after a night like that, six-thirty comes awfully early.

It was close to noon, plenty of time to grab a quick wink before picking up the kids. The rewrite on the novel could wait one more day. Brenna's problems could wait one more day.

Then the phone rang.

I picked it up, and said, "Hello?"

I could hear someone having hysterics in the background. Screaming, crying. It was not a soothing sound. "Hello?" I shouted into the phone.

"E.J.! Oh, God, E.J.!"

"Brenna? Is that you? What's going on?"

"Oh, God, E.J.! Get over here quick! Something's happened to Lorabell! Something awful!"

The line went dead in my hands.

Six

The something awful was precisely that. Awful.

Not knowing what was going on, but thinking something awful deserved immediate attention by authorities, I'd called Luna before I'd left the house, and she had passed on the word to the sheriff's department.

That's why, when I got to the little gingerbread house in Swamp Creek, there wasn't a lot of room to park. An ambulance, three sheriff's department cars, and Luna's unmarked squad car were in and around the small driveway, blocking both Mrs. Conrad's antiquated 1972 Ford LTD and Brenna's used-to-be-new, used-to-be-mine, station wagon.

I parked two houses down and jogged to Brenna's house, vowing to start an exercise program just as soon as spring sprang. Luna met me at the door.

"Where's Brenna?" I asked.

Luna move aside and discreetly pointed her head to a corner of the room where Brenna stood with her back up against the wall, her arms rigidly at her sides.

There were ripped grocery bags on the floor—fruits and vegetables, boxes of prepared goods, and paper products scattered the floor.

I could still hear the hysteria I'd heard on the phone, but farther away now. It seemed to be coming from one of the bedrooms.

"The grandmother?" I asked Luna.

Luna nodded. "She's really out of it."

And I could see why.

Lori Tyler was still in her makeshift bed on the couch of the tiny living room. An old quilt and a floral sheet were pushed down to her feet, revealing her body clad in a too-small lacy negligee. Black and frilly, obviously something from her past life. Another floral sheet was under her. It, and the pillow under Lori's head, were soaked with blood. There was a bullet hole in her forehead, squarely between her bloodshot blue eyes.

I walked over to Brenna and put my arms around her. Her body stiffened under my touch. I put my arms down to my sides.

"Brenna?" I asked softly.

She'd been staring upward—at the ceiling, anywhere, I suppose, other than at Lori Tyler's dead body. Slowly her eyes came down to meet mine.

"She's dead," she said.

I raised my hand slowly to her cheek. She flinched at first, then leaned into my hand. "I'm sorry—" I started.

"It's okay," Brenna said softly. "I wished it."

"What are you doing home so early?" I asked Brenna, putting my arm around her. She shivered and tucked in under my arm, holding on tight.

"My question exactly," Luna said behind us.

"I might be a little bit interested in that answer myself," said a deep male drawl from behind me.

I turned. Mid-forties, six-two, blue eyes to die for, a killer butt. Kris Kristofferson ten years ago. And I'd voted for him. Newly elected Sheriff Lance Moncrief. *Another time, another place,* I thought to myself.

"Sheriff," I said.

He turned to Brenna, who stayed protectively under my arm. "Little lady, what's your name?"

"Brenna McGraw."

"You know the deceased?"

Brenna nodded.

"You wanna tell me who she is, honey?" he asked.

Brenna's voice was barely a whisper. "My mother."

"Who's the lady in the back bedroom having the fit?"

"My grandmother."

Great Butt pointed at the body. "This her child?"

"Yes, sir," Brenna said.

"Um-hum," he said. He turned to Luna and draped his arm lightly over her shoulder, walking her toward the door. Within seconds, Luna was gone.

Sheriff Moncrief came back to where Brenna and I stood together.

"You wanna tell me what happened here?" he asked her.

Brenna took a gulp of air. "I came home from school because I had the cramps."

"What time was this?" the sheriff asked.

"About eleven-thirty, I guess. That's what time I'm supposed to have my lunch break at school. I checked out then."

"Your grandma was home when you got here?"

"No, sir. We drove up about the same time. I drove into the driveway first, then waited for her to get out of the car. She'd been shopping, and I helped her bring in some groceries."

"Then what happened?"

"We came in and found . . . that," she said, pointing toward the sofa, but not turning her head to look.

"Lori Tyler checked in with my office when she got out of prison, honey, so I know who she is," the sheriff said. He shook his head. "Seems like if it weren't for bad luck, this family'd have no luck at all."

Brenna clung to me harder, but said nothing.

"You know anybody wanna hurt your mama?" he asked.

I could feel Brenna stiffen beside me. "She wasn't my *mama*," she said, her voice hard. "She was nothing to me but a biological egg donor. As for who'd want to kill her, I haven't the faintest idea. Maybe anybody with a social conscience."

Lance Moncrief raised an eyebrow. "Well, now I see how the cow ate the cabbage."

"She done it!" came a high voice from the bedroom wing.

We all turned to see diminutive Millie Conrad standing in the doorway, pointing at her granddaughter. "She hated my Lorabell! You heard her! That's girl's pure evil! She done it, I know she done it!"

The deputy standing next to Mrs. Conrad tried to move her back into the bedroom, but the old lady was having none of that. She twisted out of his reach and ran up to Brenna, her arms flailing away.

"You kilt her! I know you did! Tell 'em, you little she-devil! You tell 'em you done this!"

I pulled Brenna away from the flailing arms, putting my body between Brenna and her grandmother's wrath. The sheriff grabbed Mrs. Conrad's arms and the deputy came up behind her, holding her by the neck.

"Now, ma'am," Lance Moncrief said, "you calm yourself down or we're gonna do it for you, you understand me?"

Millie Conrad collapsed against the deputy, sobbing. "She kilt my baby!"

"You wanna tell me why you say that, ma'am?" the sheriff asked.

"You heard her! She hated my Lorabell! Her own flesh-and-blood mama!"

"That don't mean she killed her, ma'am."

"She did it! I know she did it!"

"Grandma—" Brenna had tears in her eyes, looking at the hatred coming from the woman who had raised her.

"Stop it, Mrs. Conrad," I said. "I understand you're grief-stricken. Anyone can understand that. But just stop this now. You've already said things you're going to regret."

"I don't regret nothing!" she said, looking at me. " 'Cept you coming in our lives! If you'da just let Brenna die, my Lorabell'd be alive!"

I'm not proud of the retorts that came to my mind at that moment; I am, however, proud that I let none of them escape my lips. I wanted to just reach out my hand and squash her like a bug. But I didn't do that either.

I turned to Brenna. "Honey, pack a bag. You're going home with me." I turned to Sheriff Great Butt, too mad to even think, at that moment anyway, of batting my eyelashes. "I'm taking Brenna to my house. She can't stay here. That's okay, isn't it?"

"Leave your phone number and address with my deputy, Miz Pugh—I think you're right. The girl doesn't have any business staying here."

"Where am I supposed to go?" Millie Conrad wailed. "Y'all aren't gonna leave me here with my baby's blood scattered everywhere, are you?"

"I suggest you check into a motel," I said, then followed Brenna into her bedroom.

On the way home, I used the cell phone to call Vera and ask her to pick up the kids, then drove straight to the house. Brenna was silent in the car, staring out the window. After I pulled in the driveway and shut off the engine, I reached over and squeezed Brenna's hand. "You okay, honey?" I asked.

Brenna sighed then looked at me. "Yeah, I guess. E.J.?"

"Yeah, honey?"

"I'm not sorry she's dead."

What could I say? In a way, I didn't blame her. But what a sad thought, to lose your mother and have nothing to grieve. I squeezed her hand again and said nothing.

*   *   *

I'd had Vera call Willis, and he beat her to the house by half an hour. We set up a camping cot in the girls' room and I cleaned out a drawer in their dresser and part of their closet for Brenna's clothes.

"We'll drive back to the house later and pick up the station wagon," Willis told Brenna. "Maybe in a couple of days. Whenever you're ready to go back to school."

"I'm going back to school tomorrow," Brenna said, sitting down on the stiff cot. "I've got an English test tomorrow that's a prelim to the PSATs. I'm not missing it."

I sat down next to her. "Honey, listen—"

"No, E.J. There's no point. Look"—she looked at both Willis and me. "I've got a job to do and that's to go to school. I'm taking the PSATs this year so I'll be ready for the SATs next year. And I've got to make the highest grades in the school. Because I've got to win scholarships. Lots of scholarships. And I've got to start now. Do you understand?"

We both nodded our heads.

"Well, we'll let you unpack," I said, and ushered Willis out of the room.

Once in the living room, Willis said, "Honey, this isn't gonna work!"

"What's not going to work?"

"We haven't got the room for another kid! She's a teenager. She needs her privacy. She can't share a room with Megan and Bessie indefinitely."

"You want her to share a room with Graham?"

"Don't be ridiculous."

I sighed. "Willis, what am I supposed to do?"

He shrugged as we heard Vera's Chrysler pull into the driveway.

Vera came in the back door, sans kids.

"Gotta while before I pick the little monsters up," she said. "Now, tell me what's going on."

We sat on the sofa in the living room, and I explained the situation.

"I gotta ask," Vera said. "Is this just a temporary thing? Is that Millie Conrad gonna take the girl back when she cools off, or what?"

"Or what," I answered. "She's probably afraid Brenna will slit her throat in her sleep."

Vera snorted her opinion of that comment. "The woman's not right, E.J. Look at what her grown child did and that will tell you a lot about the mother. So," she said, straightening her skirt, "where's the girl gonna go?"

Willis looked at me and grimaced. "Here, I guess," he said. "Although we haven't figured out yet which rafter we're going to swing her from."

"That's what I thought would probably happen. So, you're gonna move Graham outta his room and make him sleep on the floor in your bedroom, or make him camp out in the living room, or move Brenna in with the girls, or some such tomfoolery, am I right?"

"Vera, what else can we do?" I asked, visualizing the new living conditions, but knowing it could be done.

"I got that extra room I been using as a sewing room. That room you and Dusty used to share, Willis."

"Mom, we can't ask you—"

"I don't recollect anyone asking me anything, boy. I do believe this was my very own idea."

"Vera—"

"What's wrong with it? The girl's used to living with old ladies. And, even if I do say so myself, I gotta be a tad easier to get along with than that Millie Conrad."

"Vera, this is a teenage girl—"

"Honey, I raised two teenage boys. I lived through the experience. Might be nice to have a young girl around."

Willis grinned and shook his head. He knelt in front of his mother. "Mom, you are a wonder," he said.

"'Bout time you noticed," Vera replied. "Now call that girl downstairs, E.J."

I went to the stairway and called up to Brenna, asking her to join us in the living room.

When she did, Vera said, "Now, honey, you don't have to say yes to this or nothing. This is just a thought. Something for you to think on the next couple of days. Willis and E.J.'s house is pretty much full with kids while I got me a totally empty bedroom at my house. And I live right there in Codderville, where you go to school. Actually, only 'bout a quarter mile from the high school. If that old wagon they gave you were to conk out, which is more than a possibility, you could walk or I could get you there real easy. So what I'm saying is, you're more than welcome to come stay with me long as we can both stand each other." Vera smiled at Brenna. "And that's as formal an invitation as your liable to get outta me, honey."

Brenna looked at Vera, then at Willis, then at me. Then she burst into tears and ran for the stairs.

Brenna and I huddled on the king-size bed in the master bedroom, sharing a pint of Ben & Jerry's Cherry Garcia with two spoons. The kids were in bed, the girls excited to be sharing a room, even very temporarily, with Brenna. Graham had spent most of the evening bringing things down from his room to show her. Ah, young love. But they were now in bed and Willis was settled in front of the TV. And now it was time to talk.

"You know my earliest memory?" Brenna asked me.

I shook my head.

"In the emergency room with my mother. I was about three, I guess. She had a broken arm. But with her good arm, she held me next to her on the examining table. Curled up in her good arm. I could see my daddy through a window talking to a policeman. This was my real daddy, not David. I guess this was right before she left him."

"Brenna—"

"Oh, God, E.J., don't say you're sorry. If you say you're sorry, I swear I'll scream."

"Okay," I said, and dived back into the Cherry Garcia.

"I spent half the afternoon trying to remember good things about my mother," Brenna said. "That's the only memory I could come up with."

"She loved—"

"Don't say it," Brenna said. "She didn't love me. Or if she did, she didn't love me enough. And she sure as hell didn't love Branson enough. David could have done that to me, at any time. But I was old enough to figure out what he wanted. Branson wasn't." She was quiet for a moment, then said, "I should have protected him."

"How?" I asked.

She shook her head and stuck her spoon sharply into the ice cream, moving to the far side of the king-size bed. "I could have done something!"

"What?" I asked.

"I don't know!" she shouted. "Something!"

"Brenna, you were seven years old. Almost the same age as my girls. What could they do, those two little girls, what could they do to stop Willis if he decided to hurt Graham? Or me?"

"Nobody loved Branson," she said, her voice barely above a whisper, tears slurring her words. "Not even me."

"Brenna—"

"I thought he was a baby. Just a big baby. He could never do what he was supposed to do. He was always making David hurt him—"

I grabbed her by the arm. "Brenna, listen to yourself! Making David hurt him!"

She nodded, tears splashing in her lap. "I know. When I say it out loud, I hear it. But"—she pointed at her head—"it's in here, E.J. You don't know what it was like. All of us ganging up on Branson—"

"Brenna—"

She turned to look at me, and the anguish on her face almost stopped my heart from beating. "E.J., I held the tape."

"What?"

"That night. The night they killed him. I held the duct

tape for David while he taped the blanket. I helped them kill my brother.''

My stomach heaved at what had been done to this child. I got up from the bed and walked to her side and lifted her into my arms, holding her as tightly as she'd let me. "It wasn't your fault," I said softly in her ear. "It wasn't your fault."

Willis got his partner Doug to help him move the station wagon to our house. The next morning, I helped Brenna pack her stuff into the back of it. "Mrs. Pugh was right," she said. "It'll be a lot easier getting to school and to Josh's office if I stay at her house. And y'all just don't have the room."

"You're welcome here anytime—"

She hugged me. "I know that. Believe me, I know that."

She rolled her window down and I came to stand by her side of the car. She started it, looked at me, and smiled. "Thank you, Aunt Frieda," she said.

As she pulled out, the tears began streaming down my face.

I sat in my office under the stairs, staring at the computer screen, not really caring what was happening with my two lovers in my newest romance novel. I wasn't in a romantic mood.

Things have happened to me over the past couple of years—bad things. My best friends were murdered next door. A year later a crazy person tried to kill me. Shortly after that, Willis disappeared, and that whole experience ended up with the two of us being chased over a mountaintop by bloodthirsty Neanderthals.

I have a way of attracting trouble; but I also have a way of ferreting out the truth. I was worried that the sheriff, cute as his butt might be, might begin to take Millie Conrad's accusations against Brenna seriously. Brenna needed help for a lot of reasons, not one of them being the fact that she was homicidal. She wasn't. She was a kid who had every reason in the world to be three times as screwed up as she was.

I knew I was beginning to love her, as if she were my own flesh-and-blood child. I worried once that I wouldn't be able to find enough love to be a mother to Bessie when we took her into our family; now I find I have love spilling over. I've discovered that love grows exponentially; the more you give, the more there is.

I wasn't going to let anything else happen to Brenna. Not if I could help it. And the best way to keep Lance Moncrief away from Brenna, was to find out who killed Lori Tyler. Whether it was a stranger off the street or someone with a very particular reason.

For the first time since I'd heard his name, I decided I'd like to have a nice long chat with David Tyler.

Seven

The last person in the world I wanted to see or talk to was Millie Conrad, but I needed to know things only Mrs. Conrad could tell me. If even she knew the answers.

I drove to the little house in Swamp Creek, only to find it closed up and the ancient LTD gone. A quick chat with the next-door neighbor told me Millie Conrad was staying with some friends from her church. I got the name of the church—the Almighty Christ Redeemer Basic Bible Church—and the address from the neighbor, and drove over there.

The church was housed in a defunct 7-Eleven, and was shut tight when I got there; there was no response to my knock on the door. I stood in the cold, wondering what to do next.

Suddenly a voice spoke up. "Looking for the preacher?" it said.

I saw an old man's head sticking out from under a jacked-up car. Relieved to know it wasn't the voice of

God, I said, "Yes. Do you know how to get in touch with him?"

"The old fool don't have a telephone," the man said. "But he lives out my way."

He crawled the rest of the way out from under the car. "This old thing's not gonna run again in my lifetime," he said, indicating the car. "Give me a lift, and I'll show you where the preacher lives."

I'm not generally prone to giving strange men rides, but this one was in his late seventies and about Graham's size. I figured I could take him if it came to that.

"Sure," I said. "Hop in."

I started up the minivan and he introduced himself. "Ed Perkins, ma'am," he said. "Thank you kindly for the lift."

"My pleasure, Mr. Perkins. E.J. Pugh." He shook my outstretched hand and shrugged.

"Can't get real used to shaking hands with a lady," he said. "Wasn't done in my day. 'Course, in my day, ladies didn't wear blue jeans and drive cars none either."

I couldn't help grinning at him. "Thank goodness those days are gone, huh, Mr. Perkins?"

He grinned back. "Seeing how fine you look in them jeans, Miz Pugh, I gotta say amen to that."

I laughed and asked for directions. We took a farm-to-market road out of town for a couple of miles, then an old road off that. Mr. Perkins directed me to stop at a leaning mailbox next to a driveway that led quite a ways up to a dilapidated old house.

"You take this here minivan thing up that driveway, little lady, you gonna be spending the next few months there until the road dries up. Not much of a walk, and I thank you kindly for the ride."

"You said the preacher lives out this way?"

"Yes, ma'am," Mr. Perkins said, crawling out of the van. "Brother Rice Albany. Can't say he's my type of preacher. For a short sucker, he's got a long reach—right into your back pocket. Lives on down this road 'bout half a mile. First trailer you'll see on the right.''

I thanked him and drove on, soon to find out why the congregation of the Almighty Christ Redeemer Basic Bible Church could only afford a defunct 7-Eleven for their sanctuary.

Although Brother Rice Albany lived in a modest trailer on a modest ten-acre tract of land, that ten acres was dotted liberally with loot: a twenty-four-foot bass boat with twin inboard motors; a brand-new Chrysler Le Baron convertible; a two-year-old Chevy dualie pickup in descending shades of purple, with a matching fifth-wheeler RV balanced on sawhorses in the yard; a full-dress Harley with sidecar and saddlebags; and a satellite dish just a touch smaller than the one at NASA.

As I pulled into the yard, the front door of the trailer opened and a short man, about as wide as he was tall, stood framed in the small doorway. He came down the steps as I got out of the van.

"Can I help you?" he said.

He had a full wig on top of his head, one he must have pulled on in a hurry because it leaned slightly to the left as he stood before me, giving him a lopsided appearance. The wig was what a professional colorist would have called champagne blond, and, if it had been sitting correctly on his head, he would have had a little sprig of hair casually dropping to his forehead. As it was, it seemed to be blocking the vision in his left eye. He had a small mustache that appeared natural enough, and for a moment he looked terribly familiar to me. Then I realized what it was: He looked just like that guy in the "Popeye" cartoons who eats all the hamburgers, if Wimpy was wearing a bad rug.

"Brother Rice Albany?" I asked.

"Yes, ma'am, how may I be of service to you?"

"I'm sorry to bother you, but I'm looking for a member of your church—Millie Conrad. I'm told she's staying with members of the church, but I don't know where, and it's important that I see her.''

Brother Rice Albany made a ''tsk, tsk'' sound and shook his head, dislodging the wig enough that he had to grab it with one hand. ''Such a tragedy about Sister Millie's daughter Lorabell. I want you to know I been on bended knee almost every second since it happened, praying for that poor girl's everlasting salvation.''

''I'm sure Mrs. Conrad is grateful for your strength, Brother Rice,'' I said.

He looked at me humbly, then said, ''Well, now I can tell you where she's staying for the next couple of days while some of the ladies from the church clean up the— well, you know.''

''Of course,'' I said.

He gave me the name and address of the couple who had taken ''Sister Millie'' in, and I thanked him, heading for the minivan.

''Are your spiritual needs being met, Miz Pugh?'' he asked me.

Oh, God, I thought. *The commercial.*

''Yes, Brother Rice, and thank you for asking. My family membership is at a church in Black Cat Ridge.''

He frowned. ''Now, only churches I know of in that Sodom and Gomorrah are humanistic places full of Methodists and Presbyterians.''

''There's a nice Southern Baptist church there,'' I said, crawling quickly behind the wheel and turning the key.

''Them Southern Baptists are a lot more liberal than you mighta been led to believe, ma'am,'' Brother Rice said. ''Why, I heard tell they're thinking of letting women preach the Lord's word.'' He shook his head so hard the little sprig of hair meant for his forehead was now tickling his left ear. ''Wasn't Adam got us thrown out of the Garden of Eden, now was it, ma'am? Seems to me it was a woman done that. A woman called Eve. You getting my drift, ma'am?''

"Thank you for the information, Brother Rice," I said, and backed up as quickly as possible out of his yard.

"A woman preaching gospel! Don't that beat all?" I heard him say as I put the car in drive and got the hell out of there.

Sister Millie Conrad was staying at the home of Brother Jack and Sister Jonnella Murphy on Almond Joy Way in Swamp Creek. I drove back to the tiny town and soon found the address on Almond Joy Way. It was another trailer, this one more of the permanent kind, with additions—a room on the back, a large screened-in porch on the front—sitting on several acres of treed land. I pulled into the driveway and knocked on the locked screen door of the porch. After a moment, a portly man in his seventies came out of the trailer and up to the screen door.

"Yes, ma'am?" he asked. "How can I help you?"

"I'm looking for Millie Conrad. I understand she's staying here."

A look of pure joy came to his face as he quickly unlatched the screen door. "You come to get her?" he asked. "Please?"

The mere thought made me shudder. "No, sir. I just need to talk to her."

His face fell. "Okay. Just a minute. Jonnella!" he called into the house. "Somebody here to see Sister Millie!"

Mrs. Conrad came out onto the screened-in porch. "Oh, it's you," she said, arms crossed over her shrunken bosom, face hard. She turned to the larger woman standing behind her. "This here's that nasty nurse woman I told you about."

Jonnella Murphy looked at me with the same hopeful look I'd seen in her husband's eyes.

"May I speak with Mrs. Conrad alone for a moment?" I asked the couple.

"Why sure," Mr. Murphy said, grabbing his wife's arm and leading her inside the trailer. "Take all the time you need." He shut the door behind him. I half wondered if he would throw a bolt locking his guest out, but I didn't hear anything.

I opened the screen door and went onto the porch. Uncomfortable willow-reed chairs and a matching love seat were placed on the porch. Mrs. Conrad and I both sat down gingerly.

"What do you want?" Mrs. Conrad asked.

"I just wanted to say how sorry I am about your daughter."

"Humph," she said.

"And to let you know Brenna's okay."

"Humph," she said again.

"Do you want to know where she is?" I asked.

"Long as she's far away from me, I don't care. I know where she oughta me, though! She oughta be in a jail cell or in hell! That's where she oughta be!" Mrs. Conrad said.

I crossed my arms over my own chest, either to keep myself from hitting her or from jumping up and running as far away from the old biddy as I could get—I'm not sure which.

"Mrs. Conrad, the reason I'm here is to find out how to get in touch with David Tyler."

"I knew you didn't come all this way to check on my health, I can tell you that much!"

"Do you know how I can reach him?" I asked.

"I wouldn't tell you if I did! She wanna go live with her daddy now? She done kilt her mama—she going for both of 'em?"

"No. Brenna most certainly doesn't want to go live with David Tyler. And he isn't her father."

"Humph."

"Where can I reach him?"

"I don't know!"

"Did Lori have his number?"

Tears sprang to Mrs. Conrad's eyes. "Don't you speak my child's name! You evil woman you! You done took in that she-devil child kilt her own mama, and you don't got no right saying my child's name!"

"Mrs. Conrad, listen to me! Brenna didn't kill your daughter! She was angry and upset with Lorabell, and she had every right to be! But she didn't kill her!"

Millie Conrad stood up. "Get away from me! You're as bad as she is! I bet you talked her into doing it, didn't you? That's it, I'll bet! You wanted that girl for your own evil reasons and you hypnotized her into killing her own mother! I read about this kinda thing! I seen it on TV!"

She held up her two index fingers in the sign of the cross, holding her arms straight out away from her body. "Stay away from me! You take your evil eye and get!"

She ran to the door of the trailer, fiddled with the latch for a moment, and then scurried inside.

I sat back on the willow-reed chair and sighed. *Well, I* thought. *I've been accused of a lot of things in my day, but that was definitely a first.* I got up and walked to my van, wondering what more I could do with my new magical, witchy powers.

Willis nuzzled my ear as we lay in bed later that night. "You may have your way with me, spawn of the devil," he said.

I elbowed him. "This isn't funny," I said.

"Yes, it is," he said, tongue in ear.

I rolled him over and leaned my elbows on his chest. "Ouch," he said.

"The woman's insane," I said.

"Get your elbows off my manly chest," he said. I did, cuddling under his arm. "I think we already were aware of that," he said. "I mean, that Millie Conrad's insane."

"What if the sheriff starts paying attention to her?"

"Hum," Willis said. "Could happen. Our new sheriff doesn't look especially bright."

Obviously we'd canceled out each other's votes. "Willis, I'm worried about Brenna."

"No, shit," he said. "Honey, you seem to stay worried about that kid."

"Well, duh," I said, sarcasm raising its ugly head. I sat

up and looked down at him. "The first time I see her she's trying—and succeeding I might add—to jump off a bridge; then I find out about what those boys did to her, then who her parents are. Then! Then! Her mother wants to take her to live with that brute David Tyler! And then!"

"Whoa, babe," he said. "You're getting too excited to sleep. And not the good kind of excited."

"You're a disgusting pig," I said.

He grinned. "Yeah, but you like that."

"You just want me to shut up so you can have your way with me," I accused.

"Yep," he said.

"Okay."

I woke up around three, thinking about David Tyler. That's when I realized I was still naked. I rooted around in the bedcovers until I found my nightgown and slipped it on. When you have three small children it's not at all unusual to have nocturnal visitors.

The vision of the man I'd seen with Lori at the Burger Hut, such a short time before her death, sprang to my mind. Who was he?

I tried to remember pictures of David Tyler from the newspapers and the TV news coverage. And I drew a total blank. I couldn't for the life of me remember what the man looked like.

Strangely, I could remember his voice perfectly from his thirty-second sound bites on the TV news. I remember the voice because it had sickened me. Not that it was a terrible or gruesome voice—just the opposite. It was soft, deep, gravelly—the kind of voice a woman might want to have lulling her to sleep in her bed. And having a thought like that about a man like David Tyler made me want to turn to celibacy.

That's why, I suppose, I remembered the voice.

I tried to visualize the photo opportunities the newspapers had taken full advantage of. Lori and David walking up the steps of the courthouse, attorneys in tow. David walking out of court the day he'd been released—his hand up, covering his face from the cameras.

But there had been the photo the media had used over and over—the family portrait of Lori and David and the two children. I could remember Branson Lee so clearly in my mind: a little paler than the rest of the family, freckles cresting his nose, hair not quite as dark as his sister's. He wasn't smiling in the picture. A lot had been made in the media about the fact that Branson Lee McGraw had not been smiling in the family portrait.

But I couldn't picture David. Or Lori.

I hadn't recognized Lori when I first met her, but she'd changed considerably after nine years of prison life.

Could the man Lori had been with at the Burger Hut have been David Tyler? Was he that close to Brenna? And if it had been Tyler, then he had been in the vicinity shortly before Lori's death.

The only thing I'd done to locate David Tyler was to ask Millie Conrad what she knew. And that had proved to be both fruitless and spooky, to say the least. But I hadn't tried the most obvious thing.

I got up and slipped out of the bedroom, going downstairs to use the kitchen phone. I dialed long-distance for the Houston area code and asked for a listing in Houston for David Tyler. They had none.

Lori had said David was in Houston. Maybe it was an unlisted number. Didn't the operator usually say that the number was unlisted in that case? This operator had said there was *no* listing for David Tyler. Maybe it was because I'd asked for Houston. I called the operator back and asked for listings under that name in Cypress-Fairbanks, the Houston suburb where David and Lori had lived when Branson had been killed.

There was no listing.

I had been raised in Houston. I knew that the city was huge, but there were also a lot of bedroom communities, former small towns, satelliting the city. He could be in any of those towns, and Lori might easily have said, "He lives in Houston.'' But it could be Clear Lake or The Woodlands or Humble or even Sugarland. I called the information operator back.

"What city please?" she asked.

"Well, I'm not sure. Is there anyway you could find a name that could be in a suburb of Houston, but I'm not sure which one?"

"If it's in the area code, I can do a search that way," she said.

"Great. David Tyler," I said.

"One moment please."

She came back on the line with two David Tylers, one in League City and one in Kingwood. I took down both numbers.

Then sat and stared at them. It was almost four in the morning. I certainly wouldn't be winning friends and influencing people if I started calling now. Not that I cared to win David Tyler's friendship. But I would like very much to influence him—into confessing to Lori Tyler's murder, at least.

I put the sheet of paper with the phone numbers on it on my desk under the stairs and went back to bed.

We woke up to cold, drizzly rain. The temperature was down to the high thirties, which to central Texas toes is the same as freezing. I bundled the kids up in sweaters, jackets, heavy socks, and mittens, borrowed a pair of thick socks from Willis's sock drawer, bundled myself up, and took them to school.

On the way back, all I could think of was getting back to my office and calling the numbers sitting on my desk. The newsman on the car radio was predicting a hard freeze that night with the possibility of sleet turning to snow by morning. *Right*, I thought. *Snow. My children have never seen snow.* The last time it had snowed in the Codderville area had been the year of Megan's birth, but we were living in Houston and didn't get it. I couldn't help but wish the weatherman was right. It would be great fun to have snow, to watch the kids playing in it. Okay, to play in it myself. I'm not above that.

It was about the time I was dreaming of this winter wonderland that the van, my almost-brand-new minivan, decided that it was too tired to make the rest of the trip home. It burped, sent a cloud of sooty black smoke pouring out of the tailpipe, and died.

And I remembered fondly the sight of the cell phone sitting next to its battery charger on the counter in the kitchen.

It was basically simultaneous with the thought of the faraway cell phone that the drizzly rain turned into a moonsoon.

I sat in the van, hoping the torrential downpour would let up in the foreseeable future, and considered that if I'd been married to a *real* man, he would have known better than to buy a piece-of-shit junker like this minivan.

Then I thought life in the suburbs must be getting to me and it might be time to renew my membership in NOW.

I started a fire in the fireplace and pulled a chair up close, sticking my feet on the hearth. I had a hole in the sole of my Reeboks. By the time I got home, even though the rain had slacked up, I was soaked to the skin, and my feet were wet and numb. I had just gotten settled when the phone rang.

Grumbling, I got up and went to the kitchen and picked it up.

"Hello?"

"Mrs. Pugh?"

"Yes?"

"This is Mary Morrison at the West Side Nursing Home in Lubbock."

I'd known this call was coming; I just didn't know exactly when I'd get it, and the timing couldn't have been worse.

The West Side Nursing Home was where Bessie's birth grandmother had been living for the last year. She was my late best friend Terry's mother and had been dying of cancer for two very long years. The only reason we had inherited Bessie was because of Nancy Karnes's terminal condition. Terry's father had died several years before and her only sister, Lynda, had been killed in a car wreck the year before Terry and her family had been murdered.

"Yes, Ms. Morrison?" I said into the phone.

"I'm sorry to tell you that Nancy Karnes passed away early this morning," she said.

I sighed. "Thank you for calling me. I believe there are papers in her file stipulating what funeral home—"

"Yes, ma'am. I've already called them. I thought you might want to check with them," she said.

"Yes, of course."

She read me the phone number of the funeral home in Lubbock, said how sorry she was for my loss, and hung up.

I hung up too and sat staring at the phone.

Funerals. God, how I hated funerals.

Which made me wonder about another funeral I should be going to: Lori Tyler's. But Mrs. Conrad had said nothing about funeral arrangements. I wondered if the Almighty Christ Redeemer Basic Bible Church believed in funerals or just went with your basic Hefty bag approach to human remains disposal. I'd have to find out.

Which would be a nice way of putting off the inevitable. I picked up the phone and dialed the number of the funeral home in Lubbock. First things first.

After Bessie had come to live with us, and life had settled down to its usual manic state, we'd taken a family trip to Lubbock for Bessie to see her grandmother. It had not been a good visit. Mrs. Karnes had just been moved from the hospital to the nursing home. She was very sick and in a great deal of pain. She tried to act normally around her youngest and only surviving grandchild, but as we'd gotten ready to leave, she'd asked to speak to me alone.

"Don't bring her back," she'd breathed. "I don't want her to remember me like this. There are pictures. I have a rented storage space. Everything I want Bessie to have when I go. Show her the pictures and tell her that was her grandmother. Not the dying old lady she sees now."

I'd kissed her lightly on the forehead, remembering the vital woman who had spent part of every vacation at Terry's house, arguing with her daughter and flirting shamelessly with her son-in-law.

Since that visit, every time I got pictures developed of the children, I'd send ones of Bessie to Nancy Karnes. It was always a special time for Bessie and me; she'd draw a picture or make a card and we'd package up the pictures for her own special grandmother and we'd make a special trip to the post office to mail the package.

Now the only family Bessie had left was us. It would have to do.

It was going to cost $842.79 to fix the minivan. Because of my shopping spree on Brenna's behalf, the Visa card maxed out after only $411. Which meant taking the rest of the money out of our always skimpy savings. *There goes the new washing machine,* I thought. Our appliances, like our automobiles, were always on their last legs.

The repairs needed to be done in a hurry because we had to go to Lubbock as soon as possible. Texas, in case you never heard, is a very big state, and the trip to Lubbock would take six to eight hours, depending on pit stops. With three children there were always a lot of pit stops.

Willis took care of the minivan, and I took care of explaining to Bessie, yet again, why someone she loved had died.

I got Brenna over to the house to act as baby-sitter for the other two while I took Bessie to her room. She sat on her bed, her long brown hair tousled from too much fun, her big brown eyes, Terry's eyes, Nancy Karnes's eyes, looking at me in wonder, while I sat on Megan's bed across from her.

"What's up, Mom?" she said, imitating her brother Graham, and giggling.

"You remember me telling you how sick Grandma Karnes is?"

"Yes," she said, the smile leaving her face and the light dying in her big, cocker spaniel brown eyes.

I reached across the space between the beds and took her little hand in mine. "Honey, she's gone to Heaven, to be with Mama Terry and Daddy Roy."

Tears filled her eyes. "I don't want her to," she said.

"I know, sweetie. Neither do I. But she was very sick, and she was hurting, and in Heaven she won't hurt anymore."

"Can we still send her pictures in Heaven?" Bessie asked.

"No. But I'll tell you what Grandma Karnes told me last time we went to visit. She has a storage room with all sorts of stuff she wanted you to have, and in there are pictures she's sending to you."

"Really?" Bessie asked.

"Really. That's what she told me. So we'll go get those pictures. And you can keep them forever."

"With the pictures I have of Mama Terry and Daddy Roy?"

"That's right, honey. We'll keep them all together. And we'll call them Bessie's special family pictures."

"Okay," she said. She wiped a tear from her eye and jumped off the bed. "Can I go tell Brenna about my pictures?"

"You sure can," I said.

"And I'm gonna tell Megan. 'Cause Megan doesn't have a special family. She's just got this one."

I smiled. "That sounds fine," I said.

Yep, poor Megan and Graham. The only family they had was this old used-up one. Sigh.

We left at 5:00 A.M. Saturday morning. It took eight full hours to get to Lubbock. You try explaining to three children that they should all go to the bathroom at the same time.

"But I don't have to go now!"

"But I didn't have to go then!"

"I have to go right this second!"

Then there was the pulling over for threats.

"You sit there! Don't move! You! Fasten your seat belt! The next person who utters a word gets left on the side of the road!"

And all this even though we brought Brenna along for buffer. Well, not just for buffer. I couldn't stand thinking of leaving town without Brenna. She was too vulnerable right now.

And then there was the weather. It had been in the mid-forties and tolerable when we'd left Black Cat Ridge, but as we traveled north, it got colder and wetter. Low forties and rain in Waco; mid-thirties and sleet in Abilene; freezing temperatures and drifting snow by the time we got to Lubbock.

The funeral was scheduled for three-thirty; we pulled into the parking lot at three-twenty-five. It was a much larger affair than I thought it would be for a woman who'd been out of touch with her friends for over a year, and had no family. But there were at least fifty people there, some from the nursing home, two nurses from the cancer ward of the hospital who remembered Mrs. Karnes fondly, and old friends from the neighborhood. Bessie got hugged and cooed over so much she didn't have time to think about her grandmother.

Mary Morrison from the nursing home brought me Mrs. Karnes's file, with the location of her storage room and the name of her lawyer. Along with the file, she handed me a Chinese red-lacquered box, the name "Nancy" in calligraphy on the top, green vines with gold leaves trailing across the top. I recognized the box.

Five years ago Terry and I had taken a handicrafts workshop at the community center. My project had been a Christmas wreath and had turned out so badly that I'd hidden it under the table at the community center the last day of the workshop and gone home empty-handed.

Terry's project had been the box. My hand touched the "y" in Nancy's name, where Terry's inexperienced hand had messed up. The tail of the "y" was a little crooked and there was just the slightest smear of the gold paint she'd used for her lettering.

Tears sprang to my eyes. It's strange, after all this time, over two years, that the smallest things can bring Terry back to me in such clarity.

"Mom always called me the smart one. Every time I tried to sew a dress or make a cake and I screwed it up, she'd say, 'That's okay, honey. You're too smart for domestic chores!' So my sister becomes the lawyer, and I end up a housewife with three kids!"

That box had been so important to Terry. She made it as a Christmas gift for her mother.

Nancy must have realized the importance of it. She'd kept it by her side all this time.

"There's a list in the file of Mrs. Karnes's valuables," Mrs. Morrison said. "You might want to check that against the contents of the box."

I opened the box. Inside were Mrs. Karnes's wedding rings and wristwatch, her "grandmother's ring," with the birthstones of Terry's three children, a gold-and-diamond cross, and a note that simply read, "For Bessie."

I thanked Mrs. Morrison and told her I'd check the contents against the list and tried to remain stoic through the service.

After the funeral and graveside service, Willis dropped Bessie and me off at the storage room and took Brenna and the kids with him to the lawyer's office. We could only hope Mrs. Karnes had made arrangements ahead of time and that we weren't going to get stuck with another bill. As callous as it sounds, we were always so close to broke that something like this could literally tip the scales and send us, if not under the bridge, at least into bankruptcy court.

Luckily the storage unit Mrs. Karnes had rented was climate-controlled, so once I got the padlock open, Bessie and I had a warm spot to view her things.

Mrs. Karnes had been meticulous in storing the things she thought would be of value to Bessie. The first box was labeled "Terry's and Lynda's most loved toys." Inside were beautiful, fragile show dolls and old and well-loved play dolls; a much-loved book of "Charlie's Angels" paper dolls, and several volumes of Nancy Drew and Judy Bolton mysteries. The next box was labeled "My Grandmother's china." The third was "picture albums." Each album was marked with dates, starting with Mrs. Karnes's own childhood, through the childhoods of both of her daughters, on to the births of her grandchildren. Besides the boxes there was an old rocker with a label pinned to the cushion: "My mother's rocking chair. She bought it before I was born."; a carved Chinese chest in faded hues of green and red, labeled: "My grandmother's wedding chest. Inside are mementos of my daughters"; and a delicate secretary, carved of dark mahogany, labeled: "My mother's writing desk."

I almost jumped out of my skin when there was a knock on the door. I opened it and peered out. A man stood there. "You Miz Pugh?" he asked.

"Yes, sir. Are you the manager of the storage facility?"

"Oh, no, ma'am. I'm from U-Haul. Miz Morrison from the nursing home called me 'bout Miz Karnes's death. Miz Karnes, she made arrangements with us a while back to bring a U-Haul over here on the day of her funeral. So I got it parked right here, ma'am. You know what to do with it?"

I smiled at him. "Yes, I certainly do."

Mrs. Karnes had been very organized.

Bessie and I went by the office of the storage facility to settle up, and I ended up with a check in my hands for $212. Mrs. Karnes had paid for a year in advance.

When Willis showed up with the kids and the minivan,

he also had news of Mrs. Karnes's thoughtfulness and organizational skills.

"Funeral and grave site were paid for in advance, with a perpetual-care clause," he said. "She'd liquidated all her assets and made arrangements with her lawyer to pay all outstanding bills. He said probate shouldn't take long." He pulled me away from the kids. "Honey, she left you and me the bulk of her estate."

"What?"

He pulled an envelope from his pocket. "Read this."

I recognized the writing, from amusing letters Terry had shared with me and the notes on the things in the storage shed. Nancy Karnes's hand.

Dear E.J. and Willis,

I didn't know if I'd be able to make it through the death of the only daughter I had left, not to mention my "son" Roy and two of my grandchildren. If Bessie hadn't made it, I think I would have died that day.

You get awfully selfish when you're dying. There's so much "why me, oh Lord" crap that it would make a sane woman scream. But it's the truth. The hardest thing I've ever done is tell you to keep Bessie. The second hardest was telling Terry not to put me down as guardian of the children in their will. But that was an abstract thing. The two of you actually having to take Bessie into your home was reality. And I don't know what I would have done if you hadn't been there.

May I tell you now that your note to me, E.J., telling me of Bessie's legal adoption into your family, was a mixed blessing. I cried for hours, as if I'd again lost a grandchild. Because, in reality I had. But I knew this was the best thing for her, and I bless you and Willis every day for loving her and caring for her.

There won't be a lot left by the time this old body finally heaves its last breath, but what there is goes to the two of you. I know Bessie has enough money from her parents' estate to see her through college and then some. But meanwhile, I know the two of you have been struggling with not just two, but now three children. This is my gift to you, in exchange for your gift to me.

Take care and love my baby forever. As I know you will.

With love,
Nancy

Tears were streaming down my face as I folded the letter and put it back in the envelope. Something else to keep for Bessie—until she was old enough to appreciate it for what it was worth.

The kids, all four of them, were busy making and throwing snowballs as I went into my husband's arms, grateful for the strength and the warmth.

"When you're feeling better, I'll tell you how much," he said.

I looked up at him. "Now. Tell me now."

"Eighty-five thousand."

The quiet tears turned into sobs as I held my husband to me. "I can get a new washing machine," I said, sobbing.

Eight

We might have been eighty-five thousand dollars richer than we had been on the drive to Lubbock, but probate takes a while. We spent the night in two rooms of a Motel 6; Willis and Graham in one room, and the four "girls" in a room with two double beds.

The little girls were exhausted from the drive up, the snow, the adventure in general. They were sound asleep before eight-thirty. Brenna and I shared one of the double beds, propped up on pillows with the TV turned low, Brenna in a Mickey Mouse nightshirt and me in the jammies with the feet and trapdoor that my husband so admires.

I tried to sound nonchalant when I asked, "Brenna, do you have any pictures of David Tyler?"

Her head jerked around to look at me. "Why?"

As truthfully as I could, I said, "Because I'd like to be on the lookout for him."

"You think he's coming after me?" Brenna said, her face anxious.

"No, honey," I said, touching her lightly on the arm. "Not at all. Do you have any pictures?"

"Yeah, I guess. I've got an old picture album my grandmother gave me when I was little. It had been my mom's. I've never looked at it though."

"You have it at Vera's house?"

"Yeah, I guess it's with my stuff."

"Maybe we can look through it when we get home," I said. "By the way, have you heard anything about Lori's funeral?"

She shook her head. "No, and I don't care. I have no intention of going."

"Why not?"

She looked at me with a quizzical expression. "Why would I want to?"

"You may regret it later if you don't. Funerals are closure."

She laughed. "Jeez, you sound like Josh Morgan."

"It's true, Brenna."

"She was nothing to me," she said, refusing to look at me, staring instead at the TV set. "Let's drop the subject."

"I'm a little tired of dropping the subject every time it gets near one of your many nerves, Brenna."

She pushed herself off the bed. "Excuse the hell outta me. I'm sorry my disgusting life has left me with so many bruises. I'll try not to bleed on your rug."

"I think you're mixing your metaphors."

"Fuck you!"

I wished at that moment I had the ability to raise one eyebrow. Instead I said, "Watch your language in front of the kids."

She headed for the door of the motel room.

"Brenna, as a gesture, it's stupid. Where are you going to go? You're a long way from home—"

"Home? What home? You mean the room your mother-in-law let you stick me in? That home?"

It had been a long hard day. It had been an emotionally exhausting day. The eighty-five thousand dollars had muddled my brain. I'm trying to explain here why I did what I did.

I got up from the bed, walked to the door and opened it. The cold wind was piercing as it blew in.

"Bye," I said.

"You're throwing me out?"

"No, you're opting to leave."

"No, I'm not." She backed away from the door and the wind that blew through the opening, rubbing her bare arms that hung from the short sleeves of the Mickey Mouse nightshirt.

I shut the door and faced her squarely across the small expanse of motel room. "No more games. If you threaten to run off again, Brenna, I'm going to let you. Actually, I'm going to pack your bag for you. I suppose you probably have a lot more to feel sorry for yourself about than most people, but you can only wallow in it so long. And I think your time's up. I want to help you, and I will help you. But I can't do it alone. You've got to put some effort into it. And you'll never be able to do that as long as you're so full of hatred."

"I'm just supposed to stop hating her? Huh? Just like that? Poof! Okay, fine. I no longer hate Lorabell. Gosh, I'm sorry she's dead. Maybe we could have gotten some mother/daughter look-alike dresses and gone to the prom together!"

Willis has often called me the queen of sarcasm. I think I just found my lady-in-waiting.

I sighed. "Brenna, you'll have to find some way to forgive Lorabell. Through therapy, church—"

She laughed. "Old Brother Rice, Grandma's pastor, would love to help with that. A couple of snakes and some verses in tongue should do the job, what do you think?"

I crawled into bed and pulled the covers up. "I'm going to sleep."

"Which means you have no answer for that, huh?"

"That's right, Brenna, you're too quick for me."

I closed my eyes and willed myself to think of something pleasant. Like scrubbing toilets.

"So I'm just supposed to forgive and forget, is that right?" she pressed.

I didn't answer.

"Maybe I should move in with good old David. That would be the really forgiving thing, don't you think?"

I counted toilet brushes jumping commodes.

"E.J.?"

I didn't answer.

"E.J.? If you're asleep, I swear to God I'm going to scream!"

A blue toilet brush. A fancy chrome toilet brush. A toilet brush in its own carrying case.

"Shit," she said. The light went off, and I felt Brenna's weight as she crawled into bed.

"Pugh, you're a real pisser, you know that?"

I smiled, but my back was to her and she couldn't see.

By the time we got home Sunday evening, I was exhausted. With no snow tires (okay, bald tires, I'll admit it), we ended up going thirty miles an hour on the freeway leaving Lubbock. We were not the natives' favorite driver on the road, I can tell you that. The muscles in my neck were tensed from gripping anything I could get my hands on while Willis battled the snowy roads.

Then we got to Abilene, where it rained so hard the second speed on the windshield wipers was practically useless.

We hit wind and hail in Waco.

Then, as we turned west for Codderville and Black Cat Ridge, the sun came out—just in time and just in the right spot to blind us as we headed into its setting rays.

But my new mantra kept me warm and cozy. "We have $85,000 coming. We have $85,000 coming. We have—" Okay, you get the picture.

I know this sounds callous. I'm basically a good person. But all I could think about was what I could do with

$85,000. A new washing machine; half into Graham's and Megan's college funds (Bessie's inheritance from her birth family was more than enough for college and beyond); new Reeboks without a hole in the sole; pay off the Visa bill; have steak on Sunday! Maybe even start a college fund for Brenna!

My mind was reeling with my newfound wealth. I knew Willis would want to put his two cents' worth in, which meant something stupid like a bass boat or a new roof on the house—his two favorite topics of conversation.

I'd barely gotten the kids asleep and Willis had just gotten home from taking Brenna back to Vera's house, when the two of us crawled exhausted into bed. World travel would not be how I would spend any of the money. One two-day trip and I was totally worn-out.

I got the kids to school the next morning and headed into the laundry room to deal with the dirty clothes collected from the trip. That, of course, is when the washing machine decided to gasp its last sudsy breath. With a full washer load of permanent press, still in soapy water.

I hadn't spoken to my next-door neighbor, Elena Luna, since our meeting at Mrs. Conrad's house the day Lori Tyler's body had been discovered. We have that kind of relationship. We're usually pissed at each other about something, but I still pick her boys up from school almost every day. I figured an emergency like this one was enough to bury the hatchet over, so I called and explained my laundry dilemma. As she'd used my dryer for two weeks last summer, I didn't think it would be a problem. It wasn't. I have a key to her house and spent the rest of the day traipsing laundry back and forth, using her washer and my dryer.

This is all to explain why it wasn't until Tuesday that I got into my office and saw the piece of paper on my desk with the phone numbers of the two David Tylers in the Houston area code. I was just reaching out to the phone to dial the first one when it rang.

I hate when that happens. I jumped a foot and half

expected Mr. Tyler to be on the other end when I picked it up.

He wasn't. It was my mother-in-law Vera.

"Guess who just called me?" she said after I'd answered.

"I give up."

"Millie Conrad."

"Lucky you. Did she call to tell you what an evil daughter-in-law you have?"

"Well, she did mention it, but the main reason was she found out Brenna was staying here and she wanted to let her know her mama's being buried tomorrow at three o'clock. They had to wait for the medical examiner in Austin to give his okay. Oh, and she wanted to make sure I took precautions—what with having Brenna in my house and all."

"Jesus Christ! That woman—"

"That woman is a lot of things, E.J., but she doesn't take the Lord's name in vain."

"I'm sorry, Vera. She just drives me nuts."

"That's okay, honey, I know that. And if anybody's evil around here, it's Millie Conrad. Anyway, you gonna take Brenna out of school for the funeral?"

I sighed. "If she'll go. We had a bit of a run-in about that."

"Want me to talk to her? I don't know if she actually listens to a word I say, but she's always real polite."

"It won't hurt. Meanwhile, you want to plan to go together?"

Vera snorted. "Sure. Getting to where funerals are is my only social outing anymore."

"I'll pick you up—just in case Brenna decides she wants to come."

"Be here at two-fifteen. I do hate walking in late to a funeral."

"Yes, ma'am."

"Don't get uppity."

"Bye."

I wasn't looking forward to another funeral. I hadn't been to a funeral in my adult life until Bessie's birth family died. Since then it seems, like Vera, it was becoming one of my most active social outings.

While the idea was still on my mind, and the phone still in my hand, I dialed the first David Tyler on my list. After three rings, a woman answered.

"Hello?"

"Is David Tyler there, please?"

"He's at school. Who's this?"

"Is this the David Tyler who was married to Lori Tyler?"

The woman laughed. "Not to my knowledge. This David Tyler is twelve, and if he's been married, he forgot to tell his mother."

"Sorry," I said. "Wrong number."

I dialed the second and last listing and was rewarded with an answering machine message. "This is David" and then a female voice ". . . and this is Cindy" and then, how cute could you get, together, "and we're not home right now . . ."

I hung up. It wasn't the voice. That I knew without question. And another thing I was certain of: the David Tyler I was looking for wasn't into cutesy telephone recordings.

One of the Cub Scout mothers had graciously agreed to pick up the kids from school, take Graham to Cub Scouts, and keep the girls out of trouble until I got there. She didn't know what kind of job she'd taken on.

I drove into Codderville, thinking about the money. I'd made a definite decision about the $85,000. One I'd browbeaten Willis into agreeing to. The girls, both Megan and Bessie, would start taking ballet lessons the minute the money came in. It meant more driving, but if they were in the same class, it wouldn't be that bad. They both desperately needed an outlet other than driving our three cats crazy.

Our friend Tater, who lived in the hill country near Enchanted Rock, had a bitch rottweiler, Dumplin', who had gotten friendly with a basset hound. The results were due any day and we had pick of the litter. The fence needed some definite repairs before a dog took up residence—repairs I'd previously worried about affording. I'd also worried about the food bills for a half-rottweiler. Now maybe I could do more than repair the fence. Maybe a whole new fence, one of those with latticework tops, or rock columns with cedar inserts to match the rock on the house or . . .

I pulled into Vera's driveway, forcing myself to stop the fantasies. It was two o'clock. Vera hadn't requested my presence until two-fifteen. This would give me an extra fifteen minutes to look at Brenna's scrapbook, if she was there.

She was. Brenna was wearing a black dress that looked awfully familiar.

I said, "Nice dress."

"You know it never did fit me right," Vera said, coming out of the kitchen. Then, of course, I recognized it. It was the raw silk number I'd bought her four years ago for Christmas. I hadn't seen it since. And she was right. It looked much better on Brenna.

"I take it you're going with us?" I asked the girl.

"Anything to get out of P.E.," she said.

"We've got a few minutes before we need to go. May I have a look at the scrapbook you were telling me about?"

Brenna sighed as only a put-upon teenager can sigh. "I'd really rather not."

"You don't have to look at it, honey. I just need to see something."

"For heaven's sake," she said, sighing so hard her shoulders heaved. "Whatever."

I followed her into the room she now used. Vera, Brenna, and I had spent one weekend fixing it up, and I had to admit it looked great. Vera had moved all her sewing stuff into her bedroom, leaving behind the few pieces of furniture. The old daybed now boasted a Pier 1 white-wicker headboard, and was covered in a crisp, navy blue–and–white-striped comforter. The navy bed skirt had large gold stars printed on it and matched the curtains Vera had made for the small window and the runner on the old dresser we'd painted white to match the bed. We'd made a collage for her favorite pictures of Keanu Reeves under one large frame, and bought cheap posters that we'd framed.

Since then Brenna had added a Codderville Bears pennant, some enlarged snapshots of my kids, bottles of cosmetics on the runner on the dresser, and a heap of dirty clothes in the corner of the room.

All in all, it had the definite feel of a teenage girl's room.

Brenna went into the small closet and, after a few naughty words, came out with a dusty scrapbook. It was red Naugahyde with the legend ''Family Album'' printed on the front.

She handed it to me, and I took it to the bed and sat down.

The front pages were of a much younger Millie Conrad with a teenage girl I took to be Lorabell. She had been a beauty. Tall, lanky-legged, dark hair like Brenna's down to her waist, and a look on her face that said she could take on the world.

She'd been wrong.

I flipped through the pages until I saw Lori with a man. The two of them were standing in front of a 1976 Dodge Charger, Lori with a baby in her arms. The man was tall, thin, had long brownish hair, a mustache, and was wearing sunglasses.

I flipped through the other pages, but that was the only picture of him.

It was on the other pages that I found David. Several inches shorter than the other man, stockily built, a round, cherubic face, dimples. I recognized him then, of course.

All the old news coverage photos came back to me. The cherubic face and the sexy voice of a child killer.

The man I'd seen Lori with at the Burger Hut had been tall and thin, but clean-shaven and short-haired. I remembered the bulging Adam's apple. I flipped back to the picture of Lori holding the baby. This man had an extended Adam's apple. Tall, thin.

"Brenna, who's this?" I asked, pointing at the picture.

Brenna came to sit beside me on the bed. "Oh," she said. "That's my real father. Larry McGraw. Ugly, huh?"

"Do you keep in touch with him?" I asked.

Brenna laughed. "Are you kidding? He'd have to pay child support if he ever contacted me. Get real."

I closed the book and gave it back to her. "Thanks," I said.

She shook her head. "Whatever," she said, taking the book back to the closet.

Was it the same man, I wondered. How many years had it been since that picture had been taken? Well, probably sixteen, I thought, since undoubtedly Brenna had been the baby in the photo. Lori had left Larry McGraw before her second child was born, so the baby couldn't be Branson, I tried to visualize the picture in my mind, then age the man in the photo. *Maybe*, I thought. *Maybe*.

We got to the Almighty Christ Redeemer Basic Bible Church twenty minutes early. The defunct 7-Eleven was flanked on one side by a florist and on the other by a shoe repair.

For some reason, Millie Conrad had opted for an open casket. I must say the funeral parlor's cosmetologist had done a valiant job trying to cover the bullet hole in the middle of Lori's forehead, but the results looked suspiciously like a third eye. Brenna hung back when Vera and I went to view the remains, and saved us seats in the rear of the 7-Eleven. Excuse me, sanctuary.

The room was standard convenience-store size, which means it wasn't very big inside, and Brother Rice Albany seemed to take up more than his share of the room. The podium on the small raised dais was as tall as he, necessitating he stand beside it. His fist would rise up and pound the top of the podium every other word or two, and he was seriously righteous—regarding just about everything.

The champagne blond wig was secured to his head in the right position, and he wore polyester pants and a striped shirt with a polka-dot tie, all too small for him.

His sermon, strangely enough, was on sin. Sin of the flesh. Sin of murder, fornication, and moving-picture shows. And the big one, the sin of greed—which seemed to constitute anybody wanting to keep anything in their pockets when the plates were passed around. I didn't wonder Brenna had to wear her mother's clothes. What little money Millie Conrad had probably went into the purchase of Brother Rice Albany's satellite dish.

I did notice, however, that the sin of gluttony was not mentioned.

Brenna seemed fine during most of the service. She took her grandmother's cold shoulder well, ignored the stares of the parishioners, and tolerated Brother Rice's hellfire and brimstone.

It was the eulogy that got her.

The woman who walked up to the podium at Brother Rice's signal was Lori's age, dressed in Laura Ashley, with bottled ash-blond hair and Merle Norman makeup. She carried white gloves as she walked purposefully to her spot.

"On behalf of Mrs. Conrad, I want to thank all of you for coming out today to pay your respects to Lorabell." She looked at a card hidden in one of the gloves. "My name is Crystal Blanchard, and I knew Lorabell best when we were children. We were best friends. I remember her as a loving, sharing child with a big smile and a hearty hello to everybody. I remember that my friend Lorabell never met a stranger in her life. I was the shy one; Lorabell was the feisty one. Always wanting to push the envelope, always wanting to go a little farther, do the daring thing I was too afraid to do.

"My favorite memory of Lorabell was when we were about eight. She had a loose tooth she was scared to let come out because she had a rabid fear of the tooth fairy. She'd only lost one tooth prior to that one, and thinking about that old tooth fairy coming in her room and lifting up her pillow and taking that tooth and putting in that quarter—well, that about scared the devil out of her. And I had to admit to her that she had a point. Was it really worth a quarter to have some crazy old fairy coming in your bedroom while you were fast asleep? We didn't think so!

"So Lorabell came up with a plan. She wanted me to knock the loose tooth out and then use some Krazy Glue that we'd, well, *liberated* from the Five & Dime, and stick that tooth back in with the Krazy Glue so it wouldn't ever come out."

I felt Brenna's hand slither into mine. I wrapped my fingers around hers, and squeezed.

"Well, first we tried the old string and the doorknob bit, but the door we used came in instead of out, and all we accomplished with that was hitting Lorabell in the head a few times. So then I got my daddy's pliers and I set to fidgeting with that tooth, wiggling it back and forth. Still, nothing happened. Finally, totally p.o.'d by this time, Lorabell took the pliers away from me and opened her mouth real wide and just whacked that old tooth with the side of the pliers.

"Of course it came out—but it came out in splinters. So we had to try to Krazy-Glue the splinters together, which came out this really weird shape—nothing at all like a tooth. Then we tried to stick that in the hole, but the hole was bleeding.

"Well, by this time, my mama came home and caught us and marched us both right over to Miz Conrad's house."

Crystal Blanchard paused. She shook her head. "That's what I remember most about Lorabell. She was feisty."

She stepped down from the podium and Brother Rice took over.

A few minutes after that we were released to follow the hearse to the grave site.

Brenna tugged my hand. "I can't go there," she whispered.

I nodded, whispered to Vera, and we headed toward the door. That's when we were stopped by a clog that consisted of Mrs. Conrad and Crystal Blanchard.

Mrs. Conrad was saying, ". . . can't believe you'd tell a story like that!"

"Miz Conrad, I told you I hadn't seen Lorabell in years. . . ."

"You was her best friend! To say that my child *stole* something! God Amighty!"

"Miz Conrad, we were children—"

"I rue the day I ever thought about having you speak at my Lorabell's funeral. I really do!"

Millie Conrad turned abruptly, saw us, turned another direction, and fled. At that moment, Crystal Blanchard saw Brenna. She smiled.

"You must be Lorabell's daughter."

Brenna nodded her head.

"God, you look so much like she did when she was a little girl. Before she started coloring her hair and all."

"I don't think I look at all like her," Brenna said.

"Around the eyes," Crystal said, smiling and touching Brenna's cheek. "The shape of your face."

Brenna took a deep breath. "That was really nice— what you said about Lorabell."

Crystal laughed. "Well, I'm glad somebody liked it. Your grandmother—"

"Don't mind her. She doesn't like much of anything."

Brenna turned to Vera and me and introduced us. We both shook hands with Crystal and commented on how much we'd enjoyed her eulogy.

"I didn't know Lorabell that well," I said. "But you made her seem human to me for the first time."

Crystal lowered her gaze and shook her head. "My parents moved away from here when I was twelve. Lorabell and I lost contact pretty much after that. We wrote to each other for about a year, then nothing. When I got married we moved to La Grange, and I tried to contact Lorabell, but by then she was in Houston with . . ."

"With David," Brenna finished for her.

Crystal nodded. Then, unexpectedly, she took Brenna in her arms. "She had a good heart, Brenna," I heard her whisper. "She really did." She turned and followed the last stragglers out the doors of the church.

We were the last to leave. As we headed for the minivan, a man's voice called out, "Brenna? Brenna Tyler?"

We all turned to see who was hailing Brenna.

It was the man I'd seen with Lorabell at the Burger Hut.

"Yes?" Brenna said as the man walked up to us.

He held out his hand, taking Brenna's in his. "I know you don't remember me, honey. Rickie Brooks. Used to live next door to y'all in Cy-Fair. My little boy was Kevin, remember him?"

Brenna shook her head. "No, sir," she said. "I'm sorry—"

"Oh, no big deal, honey. Your daddy never did let y'all play much—"

Brenna stiffened. "If you're referring to David Tyler, he wasn't my father. And my name is Brenna McGraw. Not Tyler."

The man, Rickie Brooks, smiled. "When I knew you you were all going by the name of Tyler." He sighed, the smile leaving his face. "Anyway, I just wanted to say how sorry I am about your mama. She was a good woman, Brenna. She just got in over her head is all."

Brenna started to say something, then stopped herself. Finally, she just said, "Thank you."

"Excuse me," I said, as the man started to walk away. "I think I saw you with Lori at the Burger Hut last week."

His face showed surprise. "Well, ma'am, I'm flattered your recognized me. I ran into Lori there at the Burger

Hut and you coulda knocked me over with a feather. Always nice to run into old friends.''

He smiled again, tipped an imaginary cap, and walked off.

I spent the evening worrying.

According to the Houston information operator, there were only two David Tylers in the entire area. And neither of them was the David Tyler I was looking for.

And the more I thought about it, the more I wondered about the man at the funeral. Rickie Brooks. From what I'd seen at the Burger Hut, it didn't look like two old neighbors running into each other. Something had been going on. He'd grabbed Lori's arm; his voice had been pleading, hers angry. She'd jerked her arm away and stalked to her car.

Something wasn't kosher.

I couldn't discuss this with Willis; Willis was never happy when I got myself involved in murders, and this time would be no exception. Willis firmly believed the police could solve this all by themselves. And this from a former self-respecting left-wing radical.

I couldn't discuss it with Elena Luna because she hated it when I, as she put it, ''stuck my nose in her business.''

I went to bed feeling lonely and abused, but discovered an ally the next day in the last place I would have looked.

I had been staring absently at the computer screen, trying to work up some enthusiasm about bedding Molly Kincaid, the spunky business executive in my new bodice-ripper, *Deck the Halls,* with the hunky, mysterious new building janitor, Tad Alexander, who was in reality the new owner of Molly's company, working in disguise to try to find out who had thrown the former owner, Tad's father, out the seventeenth-floor window.

It wasn't working. The enthusiasm wasn't there. When I actually had them shaking hands, I knew my morning's work was for naught.

Vera knocked on the back door around ten. I said a

silent thank-you to the gods that control crappy writing, and left my office to open the door.

After tea had been made and we were sitting at the breakfast table, she said, "So what are you doing about this here?"

"This here what?"

"Finding out who killed Lori Tyler, for heaven's sake."

"Excuse me?" I almost burned myself on a too-large mouthful of the scalding tea.

"You've never been real shy, E.J., about sticking your nose in where it doesn't belong. So what've you figured out about this?"

Watch it, I told myself. *This could be a trap. Maybe Willis bribed his mother to find out if I was behaving myself. Play it cool,* I told myself.

I took a smaller sip of the tea and said, "Willis doesn't want me messing around with murder, Vera. You know that."

She snorted a laugh. "Since when have you ever done something my silly son told you to do? I thought you were a liberated woman, E.J."

"I am a liberated woman," I said, a mite defensively.

"I don't believe for a moment you haven't been thinking about it."

"About what?"

Vera just looked at me. Okay, maybe I wasn't all that good at playing innocent. I sighed. "I thought it might be nice to find out what David Tyler's been up to."

"Other than killing his ex-wife, you mean?" Vera countered.

"Not so ex, according to Lori and Mrs. Conrad."

Vera raised an eyebrow in a questioning way. "According to them," I said. "Lori and David never got an actual divorce."

"Those two were still married?"

"That's what Lori said."

"Hum," Vera said, clicking a fingernail against her upper plate. "Wonder if Lori was insured?"

"I doubt it."

"But do we know?"

I shook my head. "No, I don't know, and the only people who would know would be possibly Mrs. Conrad and maybe the sheriff, but I doubt either of them would give me the time of day."

"That's true enough," Vera said, standing up and reaching for the phone on the wall by the kitchen counter, "but seems to me old Millie thinks I'm pretty cool for an old lady."

I grinned. "She'd be right about that."

"What's the number?"

I rattled off Brenna's former home number and Vera dialed the phone. After a few seconds, she said, "Millie, honey, is that you? This is Vera Pugh. Just wanted to say what a lovely service that was yesterday. You did your girl proud." She was silent for a moment, then said, "Uh-huh . . . well, isn't that just too bad? . . . Uh-huh . . . Oh, you poor thing . . . Uh-huh . . . Now don't you worry about me . . . Uh-huh . . . Well, you've got the insurance, right? . . . Didn't Lorabell leave you any of her insurance money? . . . Uh-huh, well that's a crying shame . . . You don't say . . . Well, I'll be swanned . . . Uh-huh . . . Well, Millie, honey, I hear somebody at the front door . . . Uh-huh . . . I'd better go check . . . Uh-huh . . . Bye, now you take care."

Vera sank down in her chair. "Lord Almighty, that woman can talk!"

"What'd she say?"

"Nary a dime of insurance money. State doesn't take out insurance on inmates, and Lori never did have any, 'cept what David had on her when they were married and he was working, so unless he kept that up—"

"Which he might have if they were still married—"

"Which would mean he was probably the beneficiary—"

"Which means he has a motive," I finished up. "Not that he ever needed a motive to kill anyone."

"So where the devil is he?"

I shook my head and told her about my calls to the Houston area code.

Vera clicked her tongue and shook her head. "In my day, twelve-year-old children didn't have their own phone lines. I swear, the way you people spoil your children—"

"Vera, my children don't have their own phone lines—"

"Well, honey, they're not twelve yet either." She clicked her tongue some more. "You'll do it. Hide and watch but you don't."

"Back to David Tyler," I said—anything to get her off her favorite pet peeve—the annihilation of my children's backbone by slow suffocation of too much stuff.

"Now seems to me Brenna said something back before Lori got killed about David calling her mama at the house, right?" Vera said.

"Yes."

"Do the phone records show a long-distance call received?"

"Not unless it was collect. *But,* I'm pretty sure Brenna said she heard Lori talking about moving when the phone hadn't rung, which means *she* could have called *him*—"

"Which means there'd be a record!"

We grinned at each other. "What do you think about paying a condolence call on ol' Millie?" I asked my mother-in-law.

"Seems like the Christian thing to do."

There was no way Millie Conrad was going to let me in her house to riffle through her phone records. I knew I couldn't go with Vera; that I'd have to let her do this bit of investigation on her own. I dropped her off at the end of Mrs. Conrad's street and drove to a nearby Dairy Queen for a Coke. We were to rendezvous back at the corner in exactly half an hour. Yes, we synchronized our watches. It was Vera's idea.

I drank my Coke and tried not to think what my husband would say if he knew his elderly mother was now helping me investigate a murder. It didn't bear consideration.

I knew I had no right letting Vera get involved in this. Well, about as much right as I had myself. But the thought of David Tyler coming back with some claim on Brenna made my teeth ache. I wanted that man as far away from her as I could get him, and the best place I could think of was Huntsville, Texas, home of the state pen. Where David Tyler would be anyway if life were just and fair.

At a few minutes before the end of the half hour, I started up my minivan and drove to the corner of Millie Conrad's street. Vera wasn't there. I turned off the engine and waited. And waited. Fantasies traipsed through my mind of Vera's mutilated body on Millie Conrad's kitchen floor. Boy, would Willis be p.o.'d about that.

Fifteen minutes later I saw Vera walking toward me.

"What took so long?" I asked as she crawled into the car.

"You ever try to shut up Millie Conrad?"

"Yes," I said.

"Well, then."

"What did you find out?" I asked.

"I told her what we planned, that I wanted to look at her phone bills to see if Brenna'd made any long-distance calls so I could help her pay 'em off, and you know what?"

"What?"

"The old fool fell for it. So I looked at the last two months' phone bills, and there wasn't one call to Houston."

"Maybe that bill hasn't come in yet. You know how long it takes the phone company to put calls on the bill."

"Which means I have to do that again?"

I shrugged. "Playing Nancy Drew isn't all fun and games," I said.

"You're telling me." Vera sighed. "Millie Conrad gives old biddies a bad name."

"Now what?" I asked.

"You think Brenna might have told that counselor person of hers more than she tells you and me?"

"Possibly, but Josh Morgan won't tell me anything Brenna's told him in confidence."

"So, tonight, after Willis goes to sleep, you come on over to my house, and we'll get in the clinic and—"

"Whoa, Vera! You're talking breaking and entering!"

"But it's in a good cause!" she said, the soul of innocence.

I shook my head. "No, Vera. We're not going to break and enter."

"Well, then, you come up with a plan if you're so all-fired smart!" she countered.

"I think I'll make an appointment with Josh Morgan."

"Then have a fainting spell, and while he's outta the room, you riffle through the files, right?"

I heaved a sigh. This was getting totally out of hand. "No, ma'am. I'm just going to talk with him."

Vera sat back in her seat, her arms across her chest, and glared out the window. "Fat lot of good that's gonna do."

I had created a monster.

Nine

Josh could see me that afternoon. Vera agreed, reluctantly, to pick up the kids and take them back to her house. We had arranged for a hardship driver's license for Brenna, and she was free to drive herself back and forth to school. She'd applied for a part-time job in a couple of the shops in Codderville's mini-mall and would be able to drive herself there as well. But she'd be home when I got there to pick up the kids. All I needed to do was come up with a good excuse for why I was making an appointment with her shrink. Of course, I could lie, but I try not to do that—unless it's absolutely necessary.

Josh kept me waiting about five minutes, then I was ushered into his office. We were having one of our many early springs that we get in central Texas, and the temperature was a balmy seventy-eight degrees with a light breeze. Josh was wearing shorts and a T-shirt, not unlike my own.

"What can I do for you, E.J.?" he asked, the full-wattage smile in place, transforming him from Herman Munster to movie-star handsome.

"I'm worried about Brenna," I started.

The smile disappeared.

"I know," I said, "that you can't tell me what's going on with her when she's here, but I just need to touch base on some problems that I'm seeing."

He nodded his head. "As long as we don't get into anything that could breech Brenna's confidentiality, I'm okay with this."

"Great," I said. "I'm worried that she's not adjusting. I know she has to have a lot of feelings of abandonment from her grandmother—" A stone face received that. I went on, "and I'm concerned that she's feeling abandoned because Willis and I weren't able to take her in our house. She's made comments about not being happy at Vera's."

"Did she say she wasn't happy?" he asked.

"No, she said something about home not being the little room at my mother-in-law's where I'd dumped her."

"You need to talk this out with her," Josh said.

"She doesn't open up all that often."

"You have to try harder."

Well, this was getting me nowhere in a big hurry.

"Another concern I have is David Tyler," I said.

Josh stiffened. "What about him?"

"I don't know where he is, and that makes me nervous. I want to get a handle on this guy so I can keep an eye on him. I don't want him coming back for Brenna."

"There's no way he can do that," Josh said. "He's not her legal guardian."

"The man got out of prison four months after murdering a child, Josh. Personally, I think he can do just about anything he wants."

Josh's face turned a mottled red. "He won't touch her."

"How can we stop it?" I asked.

"We'll take him to court."

I couldn't help but echo Vera's words in my head. *Fat lot of good that would do.*

*   *   *

Brenna, of course, was already home by the time I got back from my clandestine meeting with Josh Morgan. Luckily, she had more important things on her mind than my whereabouts.

"And then he goes, 'Maybe I can call you sometime,' and I go, 'Yeah, whatever,' and Marty, that girl in my P.E. class?"

Vera smiled and nodded. "The one with the cute brother," she said.

I just sat down and grabbed a cookie off the tray on the kitchen table.

"Right," Brenna said. "Well, Marty goes, 'Better call her quick. Her dance card's filling up!' " Brenna beamed. "Just like that! It was great!"

"What did he say?" I asked.

"He just grinned and said, 'Always room for one more?' Like a question. Get it?"

Vera looked blank. "That's not dirty, is it?" she asked.

"No, Vera," I said, picking up a second cookie—they were chocolate chip. "I think he likes her."

Brenna beamed brighter. "You think?"

"Duh," I said, and we all laughed.

"Well, who's his daddy?" Vera asked.

Brenna rolled her eyes. "Miss Vera, I don't care who his daddy is!"

"Humph," she said, "well that's what I'm here for. What's his name?"

"Trent Mosher," Brenna said.

Vera's eyes got round. "Like in Mosher Chevrolet?"

Brenna shrugged. "I guess."

Vera stood, taking the cookie plate to the cookie jar. "Well, now, seems to me either Willis or Dusty went to school with the Mosher boy who's running the dealership now. E.J., you ask Willis if he knows the daddy, okay?"

"Gawd, Miss Vera! Sure you don't want to get his Dun & Bradstreet?"

"His what, honey?"

Since Vera's back was to me, I made a motion with my hand over my head. Unfortunately, Vera turned.

"I saw that!" she said.

Brenna jumped up and kissed Vera on the cheek. "We love you even if you don't get all our incredibly witty jokes!"

"Ha! If they were all that witty, seems to me y'all couldn't think of 'em!"

"Well," I said, seeing as the cookies were put away, "I suppose I should get the kids home and try to come up with something creative for Willis's dinner."

"Oh, honey; don't try creative," Vera said. "A Popsicle stick in some frozen hamburger meat'll seem gourmet to my son."

I kissed them both on cheeks, grabbed my offspring, and headed home.

It was eight o'clock, the girls were in bed, Graham was upstairs "doing his homework" (a euphemism for reading comic books and the girlie magazines I just know he hoards up there somewhere), Willis was in the living room getting his weekly dose of "Seinfeld," and I was on the phone in the kitchen having a clandestine meeting with my mother-in-law.

"So you didn't get into the files?" Vera asked, that peculiarly Vera sound to her voice that let me know I was again wanting in some area.

"Vera, I told you I wasn't going to try that."

"Well, whatever," she said. Silence ensued.

"But I will tell you," I said, trying to again gain favor, "that Josh seems as upset by all this as we are."

"Humph," she said.

"What's that supposed to mean?"

"Nothing."

"Well, fine," I said. "Vera, I could be washing dishes, you know!"

"Like using a dishwasher is actually washing dishes. If

you knew the number of dishes I've washed in my lifetime with good old soap, water, and elbow grease—''

''Is that really the point?'' I asked.

''All I'm saying is that Josh Morgan being upset doesn't get the job done, Miss Priss.''

''All *I'm* saying,'' I said, ''is that at least we have another person on our side.''

''Somebody else who can wring their hands and wail when that no-good David Tyler comes and takes Brenna away?''

''What do you propose we do?'' I asked.

''I already gave you a perfectly good idea, and you went and messed it all up.''

''Breaking into Josh Morgan's confidential files on Brenna is *not a good idea,* Vera!''

''Says you.''

''Yes, says me.'' I sighed. ''Talk to Brenna,'' I suggested. ''See if she'll tell you any more than she has me. To tell you the truth, Vera, I don't think she has the slightest idea where David Tyler is. If she did, she knows it would be in her best interest to tell us!''

''When has a teenager ever done what was in their best interest?''

''Once. Back in 1952. It was a Tuesday.''

''Well, I guess I'm just gonna have to call up Jay Leno and let him know what a comedian we got living right here in Texas! I'm hanging up now,'' she said.

''Talk to Brenna.''

''I'll think about it.''

''Bye, you mean old woman,'' I said.

''Watch your mouth. Goodbye.''

I put the phone down, cupped my chin in my hands, resting my elbows on the table, and stared alternately at the instrument and the black glass of the sliding back door. I was at a loss.

Finally I got up and went into my office, bringing out a legal pad and some #2 pencils. I set them on the table and stared at the lined yellow paper. Who would want

Lorabell Tyler dead? I kept coming back to David Tyler, but why? Maybe, just maybe, he still had some life insurance on her. People certainly killed for that. And David Tyler had killed before. But when you got right down it, Branson's death had been an accident, at least in David's eyes. He hadn't meant to *kill* the child—just teach him a lesson. If he and Lori were getting back together, as she claimed, why would he want to kill her?

And where in the hell was he?

And what about the mystery man—who actually wasn't so much a mystery anymore. What was his name? Rickie. Rickie Brooks. What was that all about? And did it mean anything that he bore a striking resemblance to Brenna's real father—Lori's abusive first husband?

Who else? I asked myself. *Who else wanted Lori Tyler dead?*

There was an obvious answer to that, but I tried to steer my mind around it.

Wendy Beck's comments about Brenna came back to me—Brenna had wanted instructions on how to kill a mother. I'd explained that away to myself. Just normal teenage-girl angst. But a normal teenage girl didn't have Brenna's baggage—didn't have Brenna's mother.

In my head I heard Brenna saying, the day I took the new clothes to her house, *I'll kill the bitch before I let her take me back to him!*

So I thought about it. Could Brenna have done it? Where would she have gotten a gun? I asked myself. Did Millie Conrad keep a gun in the house? Surely the sheriff would know the answer to that.

But wait! Brenna had an alibi! She was pulling into the driveway the same time as her grandmother. She didn't check out of school until her lunchtime, eleven-thirty. What time did Mrs. Conrad get to the house? I had to find out.

I grinned to myself. No I didn't. Vera had to find out.

*   *   *

"You know better than to call me in the middle of 'ER'!" Vera said.

"It's barely started! Look, you have to go to Millie Conrad's and find out—"

"No."

"No what?"

"I'm not going back to that woman's house!"

"Vera, investigating a crime is not some lark, you know."

"Well, so far I'm doing all the nasty stuff, and you're just sitting on your fanny telling me do this and do that!"

"We need to know what time Millie Conrad got to the house the day Lori was killed."

"Why?"

I was hesitant to tell her why. Simply say because that way we can eliminate Brenna as a suspect? In my mother-in-law's eyes, Brenna had never been a suspect. In mine either, but I like to think I'm not quite as naive as Vera.

"We need a timetable of events," I said. It sounded lame, even to me.

"Hum. Okay, tell you what. You make a list of everything you think you're ever gonna need from Millie Conrad. 'Cause this is the last time I'm going over there. You got that?"

"Yes, ma'am."

"I never can tell if you're being respectful or fresh," Vera said.

"Respectful," I said.

"Fresh. I knew it." She hung up, presumably to go back to watching the hunks of "ER."

What questions did I have for Millie Conrad? I moistened the tip of one of the #2s on my tongue and wrote on the legal pad:

1. What time did she get to the house the day Lori died?
2. Had she ever talked to David Tyler when he called Lori?
3. Did she ever own a gun? Did Lori?

4. Had Lori been seeing anyone else since she came home? Friends, old boyfriends? Anybody?
5. Did Millie know Rickie Brooks? Did she know the whereabouts of Larry McGraw, Lori's first husband?
6. Did she have any concrete reasons for her accusations against Brenna?
7. Did Lori have an estate of any kind? If so, who was the beneficiary?
8. Any phone calls from anyone? Letters? Faxes? E-mails?

Okay, I figured with number eight I was running out of legitimate questions. I doubted there was a computer or fax machine in the little dollhouse in Swamp Creek. But these questions were a starting place. I wished I could ask them myself. Questions sometimes lead to other questions. Would Vera know how to follow up on the answers? Well, hell, would I?

With that, I got up and stuck the pad of paper in my office, where no one, including Willis, was supposed to go without express permission, and went into the living room to do a little "ER" hunk watching myself.

Friday morning was a typical day in the Pugh household. Ernie threw up in the kitchen and Axl Rose tried to eat it, which grossed out the girls to the point where they had to shriek and run around the room waving their arms in the air, which resulted in one of them knocking a full box of cereal to the floor, which mixed nicely with the cat vomit. Graham wanted to get the video camera so he could share the experience that day in "show-and-tell."

I attempted to clean up the mess while trying to convince the girls they still had to eat their breakfasts ("Oh, yuck! Not now, Mom!"), at which time Graham informed me he needed to take guacamole for thirty-five to school that day for "Fiesta Day."

"And it has to be homemade," he said.

"Why didn't you tell me this yesterday?"

"I forgot."

I sighed. "I'll stop by the store on the way to school and pick up some."

"No, Mom!" he wailed. "It has to be homemade!"

"Why does it have to be homemade?" I screeched back.

"Because you make the best guacamole in the world!" he said, his tone an accusation.

God, he was turning into such a *man,* I thought. I just looked at him and we both knew in that second that I would most definitely go by the store, pick up avocados and salsa, come home, make guacamole, and take it to his school in time for "Fiesta." Was I being manipulated? You betcha. But my heart was singing, "My son likes my guacamole!"

I have a cousin, Greg, five years younger than me, who came to stay with us the summer his parents were divorcing. I had just turned seventeen, and at twelve, he was a definite pain in the ass. As the youngest of four girls, I'd had only the dog to kick up to that point, so Greg came in handy.

He'd been there a month when my mother sent me down the street where he was playing with a group of boys, to get him for dinner. I went grudgingly. I'd just washed my hair and had it done up in orange juice and soup cans, the hair rollers of my decade.

Greg saw me, came storming over, glared at me and headed for home.

"What's with you?" I demanded.

"Nothing!" he fumed.

"Why are you acting like a bigger shit than usual?" I demanded.

He stopped and whirled around, his face red in anger. "Because I was just bragging to those jerks about what a good-looking cousin I have and you show up with that crap in your hair!"

It was the sweetest thing he's said to me to this day. Somehow, Graham's comment on my guacamole reminded me of Cousin Greg and the way I'd allowed that long-ago moment to change my attitude toward the little shit for the rest of the summer, to the extent of cleaning his room for him. He's now a thrice-divorced attorney who specializes in corporate raiding. But still my favorite cousin.

I knew from that point on I'd make guacamole for seventy-five every day of my life—if I could hear my son say something nice about it again.

I got the kids to school, stopped at the market and picked up the ingredients I needed for enough guacamole to feed thirty-five, and headed home with enough avocadoes to raise the cholesterol count of an emerging nation.

I was elbow deep in green slime when the phone rang. I knocked the phone down with my elbow and wrestled the receiver between my shoulder and ear. "Hello?"

"Well, I talked to Brenna." It was Vera.

"And?"

"And she doesn't know where David Tyler is. And I believed her."

"I didn't think she did, Vera."

"Well, aren't you the astute one?"

"Yes, I am, as a matter of fact. Listen, I have that list of questions for Millie Conrad."

Vera sighed. "You're really gonna make me do this, aren't you?"

"It's up to you, Vera. If you don't want to do it, I can't make you."

"Ha! You'll just nag me to death if I don't!"

"Look, I'm in the middle of making guacamole for Graham's class. I have to take it over there before noon, so I'll pick you up after that and we'll go to Swamp Creek."

"Sometimes I wonder how my poor son puts up with all your nagging," she said.

"If you didn't want to do this, Vera, you wouldn't. I know you."

"I do what I have to do, E.J. Not what I want to do."

"Ha!" I said.

"You know, I'm thinking I liked it better when you

called me Mrs. Pugh and I thought you weren't good enough for my son."

"I'm *too* good for your son—Mrs. Pugh."

"Shut up and make guacamole."

"Yes, ma'am."

Vera sat in the front seat of the minivan reading my list of questions.

"E-mail?" she said, raising one eyebrow. "Fax machine?"

"I know; I was running out of legitimate questions."

"Why do you want to know if Millie has a gun?" she asked.

"We don't know where the weapon that killed Lori came from," I said, trying to avoid mentioning anything about Brenna.

"Why don't we ask the sheriff?" Vera suggested.

"Because he won't tell us."

She nodded her head. "Suppose you're right." She sighed. "I actually have to go talk to that woman again, don't I?"

I nodded my head. "Want to synchronize our watches?" I asked.

We were parked on the corner of Mrs. Conrad's street. Vera opened the door and got out. "Why bother?" she said. "The way that woman talks, won't do any good." She sighed heavily and walked with leaden feet toward Millie Conrad's house.

I would have felt sorry for her—if I hadn't been the recipient of many a Vera phone call that lasted upwards of an hour, my only participation being the occasional, "Uh-huh," and "you don't say." Long-windedness wasn't the exclusive property of Millie Conrad.

I hightailed it back to the Dairy Queen, where I bought a Coke, some fries, and pulled a mystery out of my purse. I'd give her an hour. I settled in the backseat of the van, enjoying myself.

Ten

Vera was waiting for me when I pulled up at our meeting spot on the corner of Millie Conrad's street. She wasn't happy. But then happiness is not one of Vera's pursuits, so I wasn't terribly upset.

She crawled into the front seat of the minivan grumbling. "Do all sorts of tricks to get out of that house just to come stand here on the corner like a country hooker."

"Do country hookers stand on corners?" I asked.

She glared at me. "I'm a good Christian woman, and I wouldn't know the answer to such a question."

I put the van in drive and pulled onto the road. "Well," I asked, "how did it go?"

"Not a word about how I'm doing, did I get cold standing there for all that time, nothing!"

"Did you get cold standing there for all that time? By the way, how long *were* you waiting?"

"That's not the point," Vera said, her false teeth clenched. "And yes, I got cold."

Deciding that apology was the quickest way to get what I wanted, I said, "I'm sorry."

"Humph," she said.

I was quiet, letting her take the lead. Finally, halfway to the elementary school to pick up the kids, she said, "I'm better at this sleuthing business than you'd think."

"Yeah?" I said. "Better than me, I'll bet." Okay, I apologized, I might as well try flattery, too.

"Now would you call that being sarcastic or condescending?" Vera asked, raising an eyebrow at me.

"Just trying to play peacemaker."

"Well, give it up, honey, you're not very good at it."

"Yes, ma'am."

She pulled the sheet of paper with my questions on it out of her purse. "One thing waiting did, I was able to write down some notes."

"Good use of your time," I said.

"Watch it," she said. "Okay, Millie got to the house about eleven-forty-five on the day Lorabell was killed. She knows this 'cause she was rushing to get home from the grocery store so she could watch 'All My Children.' " Vera gave me a look. "As any red-blooded American woman should know, 'All My Children' comes on at noon."

"I knew that," I said.

"Humph," she said. "Okay. Number two. Millie said she herself never did talk to David when he called. She said he usually called late at night when she was asleep. Lori would tell her about the calls in the morning."

"Why?"

"Why what? Lori just wanted her mama to know what was goin' on, I suppose."

"No, why did he only call late at night?"

Vera shrugged. "Beats me." Referring back to her notes, she said, "Millie says she's got a bunch of guns her late husband had for hunting, but she wasn't even sure where they were until the sheriff came and collected them. She said it took hours to find them. They were all in the garage and in not so good repair, she said. Her husband's been dead since 1964. Must not of been the right ones, 'cause the sheriff brought 'em all back.''

"Well, this is getting us nowhere. What about Lori? Did she have a gun?''

"Ooo whee, I asked that question and she about bit my head off. If Lori had had a gun it would have been against the rules of her probation, and Lorabell, never having done a bad thing in her whole life, would never do anything that was against the rules.'' Vera looked at me. "The gospel according to Millie Conrad.''

"Visitors? Phone calls?'' I demanded.

"She didn't have any company, other than that silly preacher of Millie Conrad's. No one called—except David late at night.''

"As for your next question,'' Vera continued, "about that Rickie Brooks person, old Millie didn't have the slightest idea who I was talking about. Said she didn't know any of Lorabell's neighbors from her time in Houston and didn't want to.''

"What about Larry McGraw? Lori's first husband?''

Vera shuttered. "Lord, that woman does have problems with her emotions. I mentioned Larry McGraw's name and she burst into tears, tearing on about what a devil he was and he should rot in hell, and no wonder Brenna turned into what she was—according to Millie—what with a daddy like that. On and on. Basically, I don't think she knows where he is.''

"What about all that crap Mrs. Conrad was spouting at the sheriff the day Lori died? About Brenna having killed Lori.''

"Hold your water, I'm coming to that. It's the next question on the list.'' Vera sighed. Remarkable how much her sigh reminded me of Willis's. I wondered if they both sighed that way when dealing with other people, or was this Pugh sigh reserved particularly for me?

"She said again how much Brenna hated her mama

and wanted her dead because she's an ungrateful—well, you know.''

I nodded my head. ''Yes, ma'am. I think I've heard that refrain before.''

''Also, she says Brenna was already at the house when she got there. She was standing outside waiting for Millie when she pulled up.''

''That's what Brenna told the sheriff. That she got there about the same time as her grandmother, pulled in first, and waited to help her with the groceries.''

''Well, Millie says she thinks that's a lie. She says when she pulled on the street, Brenna was already standing in the driveway. She didn't know how long the girl'd been there. Of course, we both know what she thinks.''

''And that's it? Those are her reasons for accusing her granddaughter of matricide?''

Vera put down the paper and stared out the window for a moment.

''Vera,'' I asked, ''what is it?''

She sighed. This sigh seemed to carry the weight of the world. ''She *says* . . . well, she says Brenna tried to kill Lorabell before.''

''What?'' I almost plowed into the back of another car already parked in front of the elementary school. I slammed on my brakes and sat there staring at Vera, who was staring out the window.

''Spill it, Vera,'' I said.

She sighed again. ''Seems that night after you'd brought those clothes by during the day—'' She looked at me and I nodded, letting her know I remembered that day. ''Well, seems Brenna and Lorabell got in a big ruckus, yelling and screaming, Brenna all upset about Lori wanting to move her to Houston.''

Vera was quiet. I nudged her forward. ''Vera, the kids will be here any second.''

''Well, anyway, they were in the kitchen and Brenna grabbed a knife and threatened Lori with it. Lori wrestled it away from her and ended up getting cut.''

I sighed my own sigh. I loved Brenna. I felt about her like I did one of my own kids. But things were not looking good.

We were at Vera's house. The weather was still warm, and the kids were in the backyard playing with their grandma's dogs. Vera and I were sitting at the kitchen table, a cup of coffee in front of her, herbal tea in front of me.

I shared my thoughts with Vera—about what Wendy Beck had said and what I'd heard Brenna say myself.

"Doesn't mean anything," Vera said, sipping coffee and not looking me in the eye.

"If she did it—"

My mother-in-law turned my way with a vengeance. "Well, she didn't! Any fool can see that girl's not capable of such a thing!"

"Vera," I said, reaching out and touching her hand, "if she did, we'll be there for her. No jury in the world would convict her after what she's been through—"

"Ha! You don't watch Court TV, do you? Does the name Menendez ring any bells with you, girl?"

It wasn't the same thing, I told myself. It just wasn't. I sighed. "What about the other questions?"

Vera halfheartedly reached for her notes. "Lorabell had no estate other than the clothes that had been sitting in her closet for the last nine years. And no, they don't have a computer or a fax machine. So that's that with your stupid questions." She sat staring off into space. "I don't wanna play this game anymore," she said.

I had the first ray of hope I'd had since those evil thoughts about Brenna had crept into my head. Vera was an astute judge of character (if you excluded the brief twelve-year period when she thought I sucked), and I could tell she loved this child as much as I did. There was no way Brenna could be guilty of something like this. I doubted if a lawyer could take that to court, but I felt better for knowing it.

I smiled at my mother-in-law. "She didn't do it, you know."

Vera looked at me. "Yeah?"

"Oh, yeah."

Vera stood up and went to the sink. "Well, of course she didn't! I never said she did! For heaven's sake!"

I referred to Vera's notes sitting on the table. One thing stuck out. Lorabell Tyler's one and only visitor: Brother Rice Albany of the Almighty Christ Redeemer Basic Bible Church.

I am a prejudiced woman. I will readily admit to that. I'm a real bigot when it comes to skinheads, Nazis, white supremacists, and money-sucking assholes cloaked in religious garb. Brother Rice Albany seemed to fit that bill. I doubted the bass boat and other goodies in his front yard had come from an inheritance. He was taking the good people of his congregation for a ride, and not in the sidecar of his Harley.

How big a leap was it, however, from money-sucking charlatan to murderer? *Okay,* I told myself. *You don't even know that he is a charlatan. But,* my other self said, *we can certainly find out a little bit about the good Brother Albany.*

My fantasy was interrupted when we heard the familiar sputter of the station wagon pulling into the driveway. I got up and opened the back door. Brenna was coming in the gate to the backyard and the girls were running to her. She laughed and grabbed them both, swinging them off the ground.

She was turning into a beautiful girl. She'd gotten a haircut, and the dark brown hair shone in the sun like polished mahogany as it whipped about her face. She was one of those few lucky kids who didn't need orthodonture, and her bright smile was shining at my daughters. She was wearing the form-fitting blue jeans, lacy bodysuit, and denim jacket I'd bought her. She looked like any other teenage girl in the country—alive and fresh with possibility.

My heart ached looking at her. She would have a future.

I would do everything in my power to make sure this girl had a bright and beautiful future.

"Marty says that Tim says that Trent said he likes me," Brenna said, Coke bottle propped in both hands as she leaned forward at the table.

"What's not to like?" I asked.

"E.J., you ever ask Willis about this Mosher boy's daddy?" Vera asked.

Brenna rolled her eyes.

"I forgot," I said, which was basically true.

"Humph," Vera said.

"So," I said, returning to Brenna, "do you think he's going to ask you out?"

"Marty said Tim said Trent asked for my phone number."

"Did anybody give it to him?" I asked.

"I think," she said. "I hope." She turned to Vera. "That's okay, isn't it, Miss Vera?"

"Honey, this is your house, too. Which means the phone's yours as much as mine. Except if it's long-distance. Then we need to discuss it."

Brenna stood up and kissed Vera on the cheek. "You're so easy!" she said, for which she got a swat on the butt from my mother-in-law.

The phone rang and Brenna grabbed for the kitchen extension. "Oh, God, I'll bet it's him!" she said. She stood with her hand on the phone, letting it ring one more time as she took a deep breath, then picked up the receiver, her voice nonchalant as she said, "Hello?"

As her face fell, Vera and I both knew it wasn't Trent Mosher. Brenna's "yes, ma'am" made that abundantly clear. Then, as I watched, the color drained from her face. She looked at me and slowly held out the phone.

I grabbed it and said, "Hello?"

"Oh, goodness," a woman's voice said. "Who's this?"

"This is E.J. Pugh. Who's this?"

"Oh, E.J. We met at Lorabell's funeral. This is Crystal

Blanchard. Mrs. Conrad told me I could find Brenna at this number.''

"Mrs. Blanchard. Hi—"

"I'm afraid maybe I shouldn't have called. Did I upset Brenna?''

"Would you mind telling me what's going on?''

"Well, the reason I called. Well, my youngest is in Little League and I swear I had no idea, but one of the boys on the team . . . His daddy's David Tyler. I'm afraid that's what I told Brenna.''

"David Tyler? Where?''

"Here in La Grange. Bobby Tyler is his son. I just never put the two together—''

"Are you sure?''

"I'm positive! David Tyler came to the game yesterday and introduced himself, and I recognized not only the name but his face! I mean, it was in the paper enough! And what with me knowing Lorabell and all, I sorta paid attention!''

"La Grange. Why would Lori say . . . Mrs. Blanchard, do you have his address?''

"Yes, and the phone number. And like I told Brenna, he's working as a mechanic right here in town.''

She read off all the pertinent information, and I jotted it down on a piece of paper Vera provided, thanked Crystal Blanchard for calling, and hung up.

I turned to where Brenna was standing in the doorway to the bedroom hall. Her face was still white, but patches of dark red mottled her complexion.

"He's so close,'' she whispered, then turned and fled to her room.

Vera and I stood there for a full minute staring at each other. Then she said, "I'll watch the kids. You get your fanny to La Grange.''

La Grange, thirty miles west of Codderville, is an oil town, not unlike Codderville, built to facilitate the handling of all the oil spilling out of the great Spindletop.

Since those good old days, it has become a town in its own right, with businesses that don't rely totally on oil. It has a theater, a golf course, and the best bakery in three counties.

I stopped at a gas station, got a map of the county, and found David Tyler's street without too much difficulty. The house that matched the address Crystal Blanchard had given me was not unlike the house where Brenna and her brother had been abused. The picture of that house had been in the paper often enough, and in my obsession over the case I'd studied it.

Like its predecessor, this house was an early-seventies subdivision house. One story, pink brick, with a two-car attached garage. Without seeing the interior, I could tell it was a three-bedroom with no formals, maybe an addition on the back. Middle American at its finest. David Tyler liked to hide behind that facade. Liked to make people think he was as normal and American as a three-bedroom brick ranch.

But he wasn't.

I got out of the minivan and rang the doorbell. After a brief moment, a woman came to the door. She was in her early thirties, pretty in the way Lorabell Tyler must have once been pretty, before the ravages of prison life. The new Mrs. Tyler, if that's who she was, was a natural-looking blonde, her hair cut short and curly, with just the beginning of a middle-aged, had too many babies, spread. Her face was tensed when she opened the door—from being the mother of three? Or from being the wife of David Tyler?

A toddler of about three clung to her hip, and two school-age children stood behind her. I couldn't take my eyes off the children. The little one, a boy, had to be about the same age Branson had been when he died. Was that a look of fear in the child's eye, or was I reading things that weren't really there?

The girl was about seven, the same age Brenna had

been when her brother died. She seemed thin, tense, worried. The older boy looked at me through guarded eyes.

Or did he really? Or was I seeing only what I thought I should be seeing?

"May I help you?" the woman asked, her voice a pleasant blend of east Texas layered over with a smidgen of central Texas. (Like our geography and weather, Texas accents are diversified.)

"Is David Tyler at home?" I asked. I tried to keep my eyes off the children. I tried to keep my mind off the mantra that kept repeating itself, *My God, they let him around children again.*

"No, he's at work right now. Can I help you?"

"Is he your husband?" I asked, hoping maybe I'd found a temporary spot for him. This was his sister, and he was just visiting.

"Yes, he is. May I ask what this is about?"

I quickly wrote down my phone number on a slip of paper and handed it to her. "Could you have him call me as soon as he gets home, Mrs. Tyler? It's very important."

"Can I tell him what it's regarding?" she asked, gingerly taking the slip of paper.

I wanted to say, "It's regarding his murder of a three-year-old boy," but I couldn't say that in front of his children. I wanted to say, "It's about the fact that he's an abuser and not fit to live," but I couldn't say that in front of his children. I wanted to shake this woman and ask her, "What do you think you're doing? Do you know what he's done?"

Instead, I just shook my head. "Please. It's very important," I said, turned and left.

I drove back to Codderville, thinking maybe David Tyler had learned his lesson. One of his children was in Little League. That was normal. Maybe he wasn't home schooling them and keeping them away from other kids. Maybe he'd realized where he'd gone wrong. Maybe he was no longer the monster who had killed a child nine years before.

And maybe pigs can fly.

*   *   *

I pulled into Vera's driveway, parking behind her vintage Chrysler. The station wagon was gone.

I went into the house, finding Vera and my kids in the kitchen, busily making gingerbread men.

"Where's Brenna?" I asked Vera.

"Still in her room," she said.

"The station wagon's gone," I said.

"What?" Vera exclaimed.

We both rushed down the hall to the smaller bedroom. It was empty.

Vera looked at me with horror in her eyes. "Oh, Lord, E.J.! Oh, Lord!"

Vera didn't know Brenna's friend Marty's last name. And as far as we knew, she was Brenna's only friend.

"Maybe she's at Josh Morgan's," Vera said.

I picked up the phone and called the clinic. The receptionist said Josh had left more than an hour ago, and Brenna didn't have an appointment that day.

There was no one else to call. No place to look.

"I need to get the kids home," I said. "Maybe she's there."

Vera and I looked at each other, both recognizing bullshit when we heard it.

Brenna wasn't at my house. I called the school, hoping to find the counselor in. There was no answer.

I shooed the kids upstairs and stared at the chicken I'd left out to defrost. I should have been thinking of creative ways to fix fowl for the third time that week, but I really didn't care.

Where was she? Where in the hell was she?

I heard a commotion outside and went into the living room to look out the front windows. Four squad cars from two different counties were parked in and around my lawn. Police personnel were littering the yard and sidewalk.

And all had their guns drawn, pointed at my house.

Eleven

I heard the stampede of feet on the stairs and turned to see all three of my children on the landing, looking from me to the melee outside the landing window.

"Mom—" Graham started.

"Go upstairs. Take your sisters. Get on the floor and stay away from the windows!"

He took one more look out the window, then said, "Yeah, I think maybe that's what we'll do."

He grabbed the girls and scooted them upstairs.

Fleetingly, I remembered promising Willis that my involvement with Brenna would not hurt this family.

I heard tires screeching against pavement and gingerly looked out the window to see Elena Luna's car come to an abrupt halt, half in and half out of her driveway. She bailed out of the car, her detective's shield raised in one hand, the other arm over her head.

"Detective Second Grade Elena Luna, Codderville PD!" I heard her shout. "I live next door! What's going on?"

A guy dressed in what looked like a SWAT team uniform left formation, holstering his gun, and walked up to Luna. I couldn't hear what he said, but she turned and looked at my house.

I couldn't think what to do. Calling the police didn't seem like a good idea. Gingerly, I opened the front door. The men pointing guns at my house seemed to point them a little straighter. Or maybe that was my imagination.

I held up my hands and said, "Hello?"

Elena and the one SWAT team member with his gun holstered walked toward me. The man made a signal behind him and all of the previously drawn guns were holstered. I carefully lowered my arms.

"Hey, Luna," I said.

"Nice day," she said. "Hear it might rain."

"Sort of a hail of bullets?"

She didn't laugh. Neither did the SWAT guy.

"Are you Eloise Janine Pugh?" he asked me.

"Yes. Would you like to tell me what in the hell is going on?"

We all turned as a new car screeched onto the street. When it stopped, Lance Moncrief pulled his perfect buns out of the car, slapped a Stetson atop his dark brown mop of hair, and proceeded up the sidewalk to my home.

"I'm suing somebody!" I said at the top of my lungs. "Are we living in a damned police state here or what?"

"Sorry, Miz Pugh," Lance Moncrief said, "new uniforms."

He smiled and I forgot the name of the litigious lawyer I was about to call. The sheriff, Elena Luna, and I were in my living room. The two of them were sitting comfortably on the couch while I paced the living room. The man might have great buns, but there had been a SWAT team trampling my St. Augustine.

"Lance, I think Mrs. Pugh and I both deserve some explanation as to what exactly is going on," Luna said.

"Yes, ma'am. Sorry, Miz Pugh, but I gotta ask you

some questions. And then you and me might need to take a ride to La Grange to talk to the county sheriff there.''

Now much as I might want to take a ride with Sheriff Lance Moncrief, the destination was not to my liking. "What's going on?" I asked.

"Were you in La Grange earlier today?" he asked.

"Yes."

"At the home of David Tyler?" he asked.

"Yes, I was! What's that got to do with anything?" And how did he know?

"And did you leave Mr. Tyler's home and go to his place of business?" the sheriff asked.

"No, I did not! I gave Mrs. Tyler my number and asked her to have her husband call me. Then I came home. Well, actually, then I went to my mother-in-law's to pick up my kids, then I came home."

"Ma'am, do you own a 1986 Ford Granada station wagon, white with a red front fender and one temporary tire on the front right?"

My insides began to churn. I thought I was going to vomit. "Why?" I asked.

"Ma'am, do you own such a vehicle? I checked with Austin and there is a 1986 Ford Granada station wagon registered to your husband. Where is that car, ma'am?"

"Why?" I asked again.

"Damnit, E.J.," Luna said. "Tell him!"

I jerked around to look at her. "Shut up," I said.

"She doesn't own it anymore," Luna said. I wanted to kill her. "She gave it to Lori Tyler's daughter weeks ago."

The sheriff sat back against the pillows on the couch. "Well, damn," he said. "I was hoping the description was wrong."

"What's going on?" I asked for what seemed the thousandth time, my heart sinking.

Sheriff Moncrief sighed. "David Tyler was sitting in the Porta Potti out back of the shop he works at late this afternoon. Somebody shot him. One of the other mechanics saw the station wagon I described hightailing it out of there shortly after they heard the shot. With what he described as a cute teenage girl driving.''

''Brenna was at my mother-in-law's all afternoon,'' I lied.

''She there now?'' the sheriff asked.

''Of course,'' I said.

''Why don't you give her a call?'' he suggested.

I walked gingerly to the cordless phone near the stair banister and dialed my mother-in-law's number. Before she picked up, I hung up the phone. ''The line's busy,'' I said.

''Vera's got call waiting,'' Luna said, staring daggers at me.

I stared them right back. ''That's true, but the line's still busy . . .''

''Then maybe, Detective Luna, you could have a patrol car stop by the other Miz Pugh's house?'' the sheriff suggested.

I grabbed the phone. ''Let me try one more time.'' When Vera answered, I said, ''Hi, Vera, this is Eloise.''

''Who?'' she said.

''That's right,'' I said, hoping that her Nancy Drew hat was somewhere nearby and she'd get my drift. ''Let me speak to Brenna, okay?''

''E.J., is that you?'' Vera said. ''What are you doing? You know that girl's not back. I'da called you right away.''

''Hi, Brenna,'' I said. ''You still have that headache?''

''Girl, what are you doing?'' Vera demanded. Then, ''Oh, I got ya! There's someone there!''

''That's right.''

''Who?'' *Duh, Vera,* I wanted to scream. *Like I can tell you!*

''I'm glad you're feeling better—''

''You can't tell me that, of course. Okay, I'll try to guess. Willis?''

''No . . .''

"Luna . . ."

"Partially . . ."

I felt hot breath on my neck. "Give me the damn phone!" Luna said, grabbing it away from me. "Hello?" she said into the receiver. "Hello? Is there someone there? . . . Oh, hey, Vera. Well, put her back on. I need to speak with her . . . In the bathroom?" Luna turned and gave Sheriff Moncrief a look. "Um-hum," she said into the receiver. "Right. Well, don't worry about having her call me here. Sheriff Moncrief and I are on our way to your house. We'll probably catch her just as she steps out of the shower."

Luna hung up the phone. I was giving up the name queen of sarcasm. Between Brenna and Luna, I didn't have a chance at the title.

I grabbed the kids, flew them across the street to a neighbor's, and jumped in the minivan, only a few minutes behind Luna and the sheriff. Assuming, hoping, they'd take the interstate, I opted for the back road over the old bridge—the bridge where I'd first met Brenna.

At this time of the evening, the interstate would be clogged and there was a chance I could beat them to Vera's house.

I broke every speeding law there is and several little laws about stop signs and red lights, but when I got to Vera's, Luna's squad car was nowhere in sight. I abandoned the minivan and charged in Vera's back door.

She was standing at the stove holding her chest when I burst in the back door.

"Land, girl, you are gonna give me a heart attack! Try to remember I'm an old lady!"

"I beat them!"

"Who?"

"Luna and the sheriff!"

"Oh, Lord," Vera said, sinking down on a kitchen chair. "What's going on?"

"David Tyler's dead and the station wagon was seen in the vicinity. Any word from Brenna?"

"Oh, sweet Jesus!" Vera said, covering her face with her hands.

I sat down and took one of her hands in mine. "Vera, any word?"

She shook her head. "We can say she was here all afternoon and just went to the store for me!" Vera said.

I nodded my head. "Yeah, we could say that."

We looked at each other.

The next sound was the doorbell.

Luna, the sheriff, and I were in the living room. Vera had refused to answer any questions until everybody had a glass of iced tea and a gingerbread cookie. She dithered about like an old lady, and although the sheriff may have bought it, Luna knew Vera and wasn't in the market.

If Vera and I told the lame story we'd come up with, and Brenna came back in the middle of it, we could get caught and charged with something. If we told the truth, Brenna could be in serious trouble.

Vera came back in, put the tray on the coffee table, and I spent a great deal of time remarking on how wonderful the gingerbread cookies looked, smelled, tasted.

Finally, Sheriff Moncrief said, "Miz Pugh, we need to ask you some questions about the young girl that's staying with you. Brenna McGraw?"

"No," Vera said, smiling politely.

"Ma'am?" the sheriff said.

"No," Vera said again, sipping her iced tea.

"No, the girl's not staying with you?"

Vera shook her head. "No," she said.

"She's not staying with you?"

"Yes," Vera said.

"Ma'am?" the sheriff tried again.

"Yes?" Vera said.

"Goddamn it, Vera!" Luna exploded. "Answer his questions!"

Vera got her self-righteous face on. "Young lady, don't blaspheme in my home, please. I am a Christian woman."

"Vera—" Luna started between clenched teeth.

I saw the sheriff put a restraining hand on her arm.

"Miz Pugh," he started again. "Does Brenna McGraw live with you at this time?"

"Yes," she said.

"Where is she now, Miz Pugh?" the sheriff asked.

"I refuse to answer that question on the grounds that it might tend to incriminate me," Vera said, smiling and sipping tea.

"Incriminate you in what?" the sheriff asked.

"I refuse to answer on the grounds—"

"Miz Pugh," he started again, "a person can't take the fifth unless they've done something that answering questions could get them in trouble about. Them—not somebody else. You understand?"

"No," Vera said.

The sheriff whirled around on me. "Miz E.J. Pugh, tell your mother-in-law to answer my questions!"

I nodded my head. "Vera, the sheriff wants me to tell you to answer his questions," I said.

Vera looked at me and smiled. "Thank you, honey," she said.

The sheriff turned back to Vera. "Okay, now Miz Pugh, where is Brenna McGraw?"

"Who?" Vera asked.

The sheriff turned to me. "She's getting old, you know," I stage-whispered, and pointed at my ears.

Luna stood up. "Lance, these two are trying to make fools out of us. I know this woman," she said, pointing at Vera, "and she could hear a gnat fart in the next county. Not only that, she's not senile, stupid, or anything more than a pain in the ass. Now, this is my jurisdiction, and if you don't mind, Lance, I'll take over."

Lance Mancrief leaned back on the couch and smiled up at Luna. "Be my pleasure," he said.

Luna moved to Vera's chair and rested her hands on

the arms of the chair, leaning into Vera's face. "Where is Brenna McGraw?" she said.

Vera nibbled at a cookie and looked around Luna's bulk at me. "E.J., honey, would you call Jim Bob Honeywell for me please? He's my attorney. Tell him I'm being harassed by the police and that I'll just keep real quiet until he gets here."

"Yes, ma'am," I said, and got up to do so.

"Don't you go near that phone, Pugh!" Luna shouted.

"Are you denying my mother-in-law her constitutional rights?"

"She hasn't been charged with anything! She hasn't got any constitutional rights!"

Sheriff Moncrief stood up and took Luna by the arm. "Let's go out on the porch a minute, Detective," he said, and marched her out there.

"Call Jim Bob quick!" Vera said and rattled off his number.

I dialed the number she gave me but got nothing more than an answering machine. I left a quick message and hung up as the front door opened and Luna and the sheriff rejoined us.

"Miz Pugh?" Luna started, standing up straight and keeping her voice calm. "I need to know the whereabouts of Brenna McGraw. Could you tell me if you know, please?"

"Jim Bob's on his way, Elena, honey, and he told me not to say diddly-squat. So—" She pantomimed locking her mouth and throwing away the key.

"Okay," Luna said calmly. "Then I would have to say that you are obstructing justice. And because of that, you have the right to remain silent, anything you say can and will be used against you. You have the right to an attorney . . ."

Now, on top of everything else, I had to tell Willis his mother had just been arrested. Some days it doesn't pay to get out of bed.

Twelve

Luna didn't cuff Vera as they walked her out of the house. I suppose we should have been grateful for that.

I used Vera's phone to call Willis at work. The answering machine was on. Willis was on his way home. To an empty house. To his children across the street in a stranger's care, his mother in jail, and his wife—well, his wife was in a lot of trouble.

The question still remained: Where was Brenna? Crystal Blanchard told me that she had told Brenna that David Tyler worked as a mechanic in La Grange. Did she tell her what shop? She didn't tell me.

I dialed information for La Grange and found Crystal Blanchard's number. Dialing that, I waited through three rings before a woman's voice said, "Hello?"

"Mrs. Blanchard?" I asked.

"Yes?"

"This is E.J. Pugh. I have to ask you an important

question. Did you tell Brenna when you called what mechanic's shop David Tyler worked at?''

"No, Mrs. Pugh, I didn't. Not then. But when she came by—"

"When she what?"

"When she came by. Around four this afternoon. She wanted to know where David worked, and I told her it was for Dodson Paint & Body Works out on the highway. Is something wrong?'' she asked.

"Thank you, Mrs. Blanchard,'' I said, and hung up. I couldn't answer her question. I couldn't bear thinking about the answer to her question.

The front door opened again. Luna was standing there. "Where's Brenna McGraw?'' she asked me.

I sighed. "I don't know,'' I said.

"How did you know to go to La Grange and find David Tyler?'' she asked me.

I didn't say anything. If I gave her Crystal Blanchard, Crystal Blanchard would, in all innocence, give up Brenna.

Luna held out her hand. "Why don't you come on with us to the station? I have some questions for you.''

"I'll be there with Vera's attorney just as soon as he gets here,'' I said.

"No, I'm afraid that won't do. I want you to come with us now,'' she said.

"No,'' I said.

"Come voluntarily or—''

"Or what?'' I asked.

Luna sighed. "You have the right to remain silent—''

I used my one phone call to call home. Willis wasn't there yet. I left a message, telling him that both his mother and I were now residents of the Codderville jail. Oh, and that the kids were across the street with the neighbors. And maybe he better start dinner.

Vera used hers to call Jim Bob Honeywell again and leave a new message about her arrest. We both hoped he wasn't out of town and was good about checking his answering machine.

I'd been in the Codderville police station on many occasions, mostly to visit with and/or harp at Luna about something. But this was my first time to see the jail. Okay, to be in the jail. Any jail for that matter.

It smelled slightly of urine overlaid with Pine-Sol. There were menstrual stains on the bare mattresses and rust stains on the freestanding toilet. Except for the freestanding toilet and the bars, it wasn't that much different from my first dorm room at the University of Texas.

The floor was clean, and I pointed out to Vera that there was no dust in the corners and it appeared to be insect-free. I'm big on counting my blessings.

Vera's big on counting germs. She stood in the middle of the floor, refusing to sit on the mattresses or lean against the bars as I was doing.

That got old in a hurry. By nine o'clock that night, Vera and I had cajoled blankets from the jailer and were lying on them atop the stained mattresses. It was at this time that my husband showed up.

He stood on the other side of the bars and just stared at me. Finally, he said, "Goddamnit."

"Honey—" I started.

"My *mother*!" he said. "You got my *mother* jailed!"

"E.J. didn't have anything to do with that, Willis," Vera said. "Now, you be nice!"

"Bullshit!" Willis said.

Vera reached through the bars and grabbed her much taller son by the shirt. "Don't you be talking like that!" she said. "Now you apologize to your wife!"

Willis shook his head. "I thought it was bad when you two didn't get along. I should have known it would be ten times worse when you got together!"

"Willis, behave now!" Vera said.

"Mama, I'm a grown man, and I have a right to my anger."

Well hell, I thought, that was the one thing he had to get out of all those visits to the family counselor!

"I'm sorry, Willis," I said.

"Sorry don't shine my shoes," he said.

"What?" I said.

Vera turned to me. "It was one of his daddy's sayings. Never made a lick of sense to me either."

We were saved from any further Pughisms by Jim Bob Honeywell, Vera's attorney. Mr. Honeywell was in his late sixties, early seventies, with a full head of white hair. I had, of course, heard of Jim Bob Honeywell, the leading defense attorney and litigator in the tricounty area, but I'd never seen him. He was almost as tall as Willis, but thin, and had keen posture and immaculate clothes. He was wearing a gray wool suit, white shirt, and red bow tie. I had to ask myself where my widowed mother-in-law had been hiding him.

He walked up to the bars and put his hand through to Vera, who took it and squeezed. "Hey, Jim Bob," she said. "Thanks for dropping by."

"My pleasure, Vera dear. I would have been here so much sooner if I hadn't been in Houston on business. But as soon as I checked my answering machine, I rushed right back."

"Oh, Jim Bob, you didn't have to do that!" I swear Vera blushed.

Oh, my.

Willis turned to the attorney. "Mr. Honeywell, how soon can you get my mother released?"

His mother. Notice he said his mother. Nothing about his wife. Nothing about the *mother* of his children. *His* mother.

"My assistant is doing the paperwork right now to have both women released, Willis," he said, smiling.

He had a beautiful smile. Maybe a little too beautiful. I had this quick fantasy about the two of them kissing each other good night before taking out their teeth and putting them on separate bedside tables.

I quickly brought myself back to the present. "Thank you, Mr. Honeywell," I said.

"My pleasure, Mrs. Pugh. I'm just so sorry I couldn't get here sooner. I can't believe they would lock up a woman like Vera."

"Is anyone going to tell me why the two of you *are* locked up?" Willis asked.

"In due time," Vera said. "You got the children taken care of?" she asked.

"Luna took them to her house," he said.

"I don't want that woman anywhere near my—" I started.

"Don't," my husband said quietly.

I didn't.

Turning to his mother, he said, "But Luna came back here. Her mother's taking care of all the kids."

"Good," Vera said. "Now you go back to my house. See if Brenna's home yet. If she is, get her out and hide her!"

"Now, Vera," Jim Bob Honeywell said, "I don't think that's the wisest course of action—"

"Jim Bob, I think it best if you turn around and put your hands over your ears. I know you're an officer of the court, and you don't want to hear any of this."

"All right," he said, and did as she instructed.

"Mama—" Willis started.

"Hush. Find that girl. Then hide her!"

"Where?" he demanded.

"Son, you're gonna have to think of some things on your own."

We—Vera, Jim Bob Honeywell, and I—were sitting on folding chairs crowded into the office of Catfish Watkins, the police chief of Codderville, who had the only comfortable chair in the room. A young woman named Gayle something from the district attorney's office, Luna, Sheriff Moncrief, and a La Grange homicide detective were causing part of the crowding problems.

And I decided if Vera wasn't planning on marrying Jim Bob Honeywell, I just might divorce Willis and do it myself. The man was awesome.

"Catfish, son," he said, shaking his head sadly, "you know you need to keep a leash on your people. Arresting these two innocent women! And for what?"

"Obstruction of just—" Luna started.

Catfish just looked at her and she shut up.

"And Sheriff Moncrief, is it true," Jim Bob said, his voice so sad it could break your heart, "that *your* people attacked Miz Pugh and her *children* in her *home?*"

"No, now, Mr. Honeywell—"

Jim Bob shook his head sadly. "I just don't know that the city or the county have the financial wherewithal to withstand the kinda suit I'm going to *have* to bring." I swear there was a tear in his eye as he looked at the guilty parties. Okay, the other guilty parties. "I'm afraid I'll have to go after you each individually to deal with the pain, the suffering, *the mental anguish* that has been inflicted upon these poor innocent women."

"They've barely been in lockup a couple of hours—" Luna started.

This time Catfish actually spoke. "Shut up, Detective. And I mean now."

"Yes, sir—"

"Now, Detective."

She nodded but said nothing.

"A couple of hours?" Jim Bob said, repeating Luna's words. He stood and came behind me where I sat in the folding chair. He put his hands on my shoulders. "This woman is a *mother,* ladies and gentlemen. A *mother*! She has young children to care for! Very young children! One of whom has been traumatized already, as you very well know. Can you imagine the extraordinary trauma you have inflicted upon that child by incarcerating her new mother?" He shook his head and sank back into his chair. "The child's damages alone . . ."

"I need a bottom line here, Jim Bob," Catfish Watkins said.

Jim Bob Honeywell shrugged expressively. "Complete exoneration of all charges, a written apology, and $500,000 per, including the traumatized child, of course."

The young woman from the prosecutor's office said, "Time served and a handshake?"

"Complete exoneration and $250,000 per," Jim Bob countered.

"How 'bout complete exoneration—after they answer our questions—and a ride home?" Catfish Watkins interjected.

"Well, now, Catfish, I think all these questions of yours is why this happened anyway. These are law-abiding citizens of this county. Have you seen Miz Willis Pugh's lawn, ladies and gentlemen? It's a real mess. Someone has to be responsible."

"Where's Brenna McGraw?" Sheriff Moncrief said.

No one spoke.

Finally, Jim Bob turned to Catfish Watkins and said, "May I speak with my clients, Chief?"

Catfish regally nodded his head in the affirmative, and Jim Bob led Vera and I out the door.

Once outside with the door to Catfish Watkins' office firmly shut, Jim Bob said, "Vera, don't lie to me, dear. Please. Do you know where this child is?"

Vera held up her right hand. "I swear to you, Jim Bob, I have no idea where the girl is."

He turned to me. I shook my head. "I have no idea," I said.

"Good," he said. "Let's go in there. I'll ask you the question and the two of you answer just like you did now. Do not add a word or a gesture. Answer exactly as you just did." He looked at both of us, his pale blue eyes serious. "As long as what you both just told me is the God's truth."

We both nodded in the affirmative, and he led us back into Chief Watkins's office.

We took our seats again and Jim Bob turned to the sheriff. "Your question, I believe, Sheriff Moncrief, is: does either of my clients know the present whereabouts of Brenna McGraw. Is that true?"

"Yes, sir, it is."

"Then you may ask my clients that question and that question only."

The sheriff nodded his head. "Miz Vera Pugh, do you know the whereabouts of Brenna McGraw?"

"No, sir, I do not," she said.

"When did you discover that you did not know the girl's whereabouts?"

Jim Bob stood up, shaking his head sadly. "I keep thinking about Miz Willis Pugh's traumatized little daughter, and that formerly velvety smooth lawn—"

Luna snorted. Okay, as my next-door-neighbor, she knew there was as much crabgrass as St. Augustine in my yard, but this wasn't the time or the place. Catfish let her know that again with a look.

Sheriff Moncrief stood up, face-to-face with Jim Bob Honeywell. He hadn't been on the job long enough to know that Jim Bob Honeywell had sent four sons to Harvard on his fees from suits against the city, the county, and the state. Jim Bob truly loved to take on the "gov'ment."

"Look," the sheriff said, "there's a teenager out there who more than likely killed not only her ex-stepdaddy, but her mama as well—"

"For God's sake," I said, joining the crowd now standing, "you're not listening to that stupid old woman, are you? Brenna never—"

"Brenna left the school half an hour earlier than she said she did that day." He looked me square in the eye. "She lied to both of us, Miz Pugh—"

"Where would she get a gun—"

"Just about anywhere nowadays, ma'am. She coulda picked one up at the high school," the sheriff said.

I felt Jim Bob Honeywell's restraining hand on my arm

and took my seat. My head was vibrating with pain. It had been a very long day. And Brenna had lied to me.

"May I have a quick word with my clients?" Jim Bob asked again.

Several heads nodded and he turned and bent down to Vera and me. "Answer their questions," he whispered. "If they ask one you don't like, just tap my arm and I'll object."

Vera and I nodded, and Jim Bob straightened and turned to his audience. "My clients will answer limited questions," he said, and regained his folding chair.

"Miz Vera Pugh," Sheriff Moncrief started, "when was the last time you saw Brenna McGraw?"

"About three-thirty this afternoon," Vera said.

"Did you leave the house at that time?" he asked.

"No, sir," Vera said.

"Did she?" he asked.

"No, sir. She went to her room."

"When did you discover she was missing?"

"I'm not sure of the time," she said, glancing at me.

"About a quarter to five, I think," I said.

The sheriff turned to me. "Why would you know that, ma'am?" he asked.

"I went to Vera's to pick up my kids and noticed Brenna's car—" I stopped myself. Oh, God, the car. Why did I have to mention the frigging car?

"What about Brenna's car, ma'am?"

I tapped so hard on Jim Bob's arm I may have bruised him.

"What are all these questions about, Sheriff?" Jim Bob asked.

"You know very well what they're about, Mr. Honeywell. And your client is the one who mentioned the car. She needs to finish the statement."

Jim Bob just glanced at me and shrugged.

"What about the girl's car, ma'am?" the sheriff repeated.

"It wasn't there," I said.

"Where's that?"

"In Vera's driveway."

"The car was gone?" he reiterated.

"Yes!" I said, letting my exasperation show.

"And Brenna was not in the house?" he asked.

"No."

"Which means she was in the car," he said.

I didn't need to tap Jim Bob's arm. He was on this one, as my late father-in-law would have said, "like a snake on a June bug."

"Excuse me, Sheriff, but there's no way Miz Pugh would know that. We have established the girl was gone and the car was gone. We have not established, nor do I see how we can establish tonight, that the girl was actually in the car."

Sheriff Moncrief smiled. "Well, I got me a pretty good witness says she was."

"Save it for court, Sheriff," Jim Bob said, "if a grand jury would even allow such flimsy evidence to go to court."

Again, looking at me, the sheriff said, "Miz Pugh, why were you in La Grange this afternoon?"

I tapped Jim Bob's arm.

"Have we established that my client was in La Grange this afternoon, Sheriff? I surely don't remember establishing any such thing!"

"Miz E.J. Pugh admitted to me, in front of Detective Luna, earlier today that she was indeed in La Grange this afternoon. Isn't that a fact, Miz Pugh?"

With a sad expression, Jim Bob said, "Was my client represented by another attorney earlier this afternoon?"

"No, sir, she wasn't under arrest earlier this afternoon—"

"Which means she was not read her rights, and therefore—"

"Goddamnit, Mr. Honeywell! She was in La Grange! She went to David Tyler's house! She wrote down her phone number and her name and gave it to Mrs. Tyler!

We have already established those facts, sir!'' the sheriff said, his voice booming out in the small, crowded room.

The homicide detective from La Grange sat there quietly, a small smile on his lips. The thought of him interrogating Brenna gave me a cold chill.

Reasonably, I thought, Jim Bob asked, ''If those facts are established, Sheriff, then why are you asking them again?''

''Because I want to know how she knew where David Tyler was! We'd been looking for him for over a week, and we didn't know where the sucker was! How did she know?''

I leaned toward Jim Bob and whispered in his ear, ''I need to talk to you. Outside.''

''I need to confer with my clients for a moment. Ladies. Gentlemen,'' he said, rising and leading Vera and me back into the hallway.

I grabbed my wallet out of my purse, found a five, and handed it to him. ''Will this retain you as Brenna McGraw's attorney?'' I asked.

He walked to an empty desk nearby and found a sheet of typing paper and a pen. He quickly wrote a minimal contract between himself and his new client, and Vera signed it as her temporary legal guardian.

''But I'm not!'' she said.

''You will be by the morning, honey,'' Jim Bob told her. When we had exchanged paper for money, he said, ''Now, what is it, E.J.?''

I quickly told him about Crystal Blanchard. ''That's how I knew to go to La Grange. But she told Brenna the same thing she told me. And, when I spoke to Mrs. Blanchard later, she told me Brenna came by around four o'clock to ask her where David Tyler worked. Mrs. Blanchard told her.''

''Well, goodness,'' Jim Bob said, and sighed. After a moment's thought, he said, ''All right, E.J., bottom line. Are you willing to spend the night in jail?''

I sighed my own sigh. ''Yeah, I'll do it.''

He turned and held the door to the chief's office open for us.

"It's late, Catfish. My clients are tired. Unless you plan on charging Miz Willis Pugh with something, I think it's time she went home to her traumatized children."

"She hasn't answered my questions!" Sheriff Moncrief said.

"And she isn't going to," Jim Bob said. He turned to me, "E.J., honey, did you see anybody shoot David Tyler?"

"No, sir," I said.

"Did you see anybody shoot Lori Tyler?"

"No, sir," I said.

"Do you have any information that would lead these fine people to the killer or killers of either David or Lori Tyler?"

"No, sir, I do not."

Jim Bob turned back to the powers that be of Codder County, Texas. "Well, then," he said, spreading his arms and smiling, "I guess that just about settles that."

"No, it does not!" the sheriff started.

"Lance," Catfish said, standing, "it's been a long night, and my wife's waiting supper on me. I suggest we put this off to a more opportune time."

The sheriff opened his mouth to say more, but, with a look from Catfish, who had been a big supporter during Lance Moncrief's election, he just shook his head and headed out the door.

And I went home to my traumatized children.

Thirteen

It was close to midnight by the time I got home. A night-light was burning in the kitchen, but other than that the house was dark. I turned on the stairwell light and slowly made my ascent, stopping in the hall to open doors and check on my children. They were all fast asleep.

The bedroom I shared with Willis was pitch-black. I left the door from the hall open enough to see. My husband was turned with his back to me, feigning sleep. I know the difference between a real Willis Pugh snore and a fake Willis Pugh snore. The dainty wheeze and lip flutter were definitely phony; now, if it had sounded like a chain saw in heat, I would know my husband was actually sleeping.

"Willis," I said, "I know you're awake."

He continued the pantomime.

I switched on the overhead light.

Still, he continued his weak little snoring routine.

I went into the bathroom, ran a glass of cold water, and went to his side of the bed.

"If you don't stop pretending, I'll pour cold water in your ear."

He sat up and looked at me. No comment. No comeback. Boy, was he pissed.

I sat down on his side of the bed. "I'm sorry, honey," I said.

Still he remained mute.

"Was Brenna at Vera's house?" I asked.

"No," he said.

I nodded. "I didn't think she would be."

He wouldn't look at me. I touched his face with my hand, trying to get my face in his line of sight. He shook my hand away and eased out from under the covers. He was wearing pajama bottoms. I couldn't remember the last time I'd seen my husband in pajama bottoms. He walked toward the bathroom, closing the door behind him.

It was then I noticed the duffel bag at the foot of the bed. When he came out of the bathroom, I pointed to it. "What's that?" I asked.

"I was waiting for you to get home," he said. His closet was in the master bath area, and he had pulled on jeans and a T-shirt. "I'm going to go stay with my mother for a few days. If Brenna comes back, and she's not jailed, I'll send her over here."

"Willis—"

He put up his hand to stop my words.

"I don't want to hear it, E.J. I've never hit a woman in my life, and I never will. But if I stay here and listen to your excuses about how you got my mother thrown in jail, I'll be taxing that resolve. So, if you'll excuse me—"

He slipped on his shoes and headed out our bedroom door.

I heard the front door slam and sank down on the bed. My husband had left me. Simple as that.

I picked up the phone on the nightstand and dialed Vera's number.

"Hello?" she said, her voice wide-awake.

"I didn't wake you?"

"No, Jim Bob and I are just going over some finer points of the case," she said. I heard a giggle from her end.

"Willis is on his way to your house," I said. "He's left me."

"Well, he's not welcome here," Vera said. "I have company!"

"Whatever," I said. "Good night."

"E.J.—" I heard as I hung up.

I crawled on top of the covers and cried myself to sleep.

When I went downstairs the next morning to start coffee, Willis was asleep on the couch.

I tiptoed through the living room, went into the kitchen, and ran the coffee grinder as loudly as possible. How dare he leave me then sneak back in the house!

"You wanna stop that?" I heard him say.

I turned around. He was standing in the doorway to the kitchen, still wearing the jeans and T-shirt from the night before.

"You back for good, or just camping out?"

"We need to talk," Willis said.

"So talk," I said, turning my back on him to load the coffeemaker.

"I don't think I've ever been so mad at you," he started.

I whirled on him. "Then tell me! Don't walk out on me! How dare you walk out on me and your children!"

"You got my mother jailed!"

"No I did not! Elena Luna and Sheriff Moncrief jailed your mother! I didn't have a fucking thing to do with it!"

He stared at me for a long moment, then said, "You owe the cussing jar a quarter."

"Fuck the cussing jar!" I said.

"Fifty cents," he said.

I walked up to my husband and shoved him hard with both hands. He stood his ground, reached out with one hand, and shoved me back.

We stood there staring at each other. Finally, he said, "You shouldn't have let Mama get involved in this, E.J., you know that."

I sighed. "Yeah. I know that. But try keeping your mother out of something when she wants in!" I grinned at him. "Besides, she's pretty good at it."

Willis shook his head. "You know, she had a man in her house last night and refused to let me in."

I tried to look innocent of the information. "Oh? Who?"

"Jim Bob Honeywell."

I wiggled my eyebrows.

Willis winced. "Don't be disgusting!"

"Willis," I said, "I'm sorry. I'm sorry that I let your mother get involved, sorry that I didn't tell you she was, sorry that she and I both got arrested—I'm just sorry about everything. But I've got to tell you, honey, the thing I'm most sorry about is that Brenna is in so much trouble. Because I know she didn't do it."

"Blind faith can only take you so far, E.J."

I shook my head. "It's not blind faith. It's more than that. I just feel it, here," I said, taking his hand and pressing it against my stomach. "And here," I said, moving his hand to my breast, in the general vicinity of my heart.

"You trying to take my mind off my mad?" he asked, his voice soft.

"If I thought it would work—"

"Mom! What's for breakfast?"

We backed away from each other as the three hellions we call our beloved offspring came tearing into the kitchen.

The temperature had dropped during the night and it was barely forty degrees. I got the kids dressed in their winter clothes and got them to school, wondering if the real reason my husband had come home the night before was because it was too cold to sleep in his Karman Ghia.

I had options; there are always options. I could get in

the van and drive around searching for Brenna, or I could try to find out what I could about Brother Rice Albany. Millie Conrad could tell me some things about the good brother, I was sure, but that was only if Millie Conrad was speaking to me—which to my knowledge, she wasn't.

Who else could tell me something about Rice Albany? The old couple in the trailer where Mrs. Conrad had been staying immediately after Lori's death? The old couple who probably thought I was a witch, if they believed—or even listened to—anything Millie Conrad had to say?

Or Keith Reynolds, the minister of my church. Didn't all these guys know each other? At least he would have heard something. but Keith wasn't much of a gossip.

But his wife was.

I got in the van and quickly drove to the parsonage of the Black Cat Ridge United Methodist Church. The parsonage was on the less expensive end of the subdivision but had still taken everything the congregation could muster to buy. It was a three-bedroom, two-bath with formals, and a kitchen with a great room. It was a nice house and fit the lifestyle of a young couple.

Knowing Robin Reynolds had a nine-month-old baby in the house, I knocked on the door rather than ringing the bell. There was nothing worse than a doorbell ringing three minutes after the little darlings had finally dropped off to sleep.

When Bessie's birth parents had been alive, Willis and I had been active in the church owing to their influence. We'd gone almost every Sunday, sat on boards, committees, and what have you. We haven't been as active as we should since then. The kids still went to Sunday school, and we would make it to church once or twice a month. But I must confess, since Brenna's involvement in my life, I hadn't been going. That's why it came as somewhat of a shock when Robin Reynolds opened the door.

"My God, you're pregnant again!" I said, the words popping out before I had a chance to stop them.

Robin put a hand on her swollen belly, her back slightly

arched from the strain, and grimaced. "Is that what this is? I thought it was just bad indigestion."

She opened the door wider, and I closed it behind me, following her into the great room.

Shortly after Keith and Robin had taken over the parsonage two years before, we'd been invited over for a get-together with some of the other movers and shakers in the church. The great room had been decorated in early American, with antique quilts hanging on the walls, reproduction Shaker furniture, brass pots, wicker baskets, and lots (oh, my Lord, *lots*) of silk flower and wrinkle ribbon arrangements. Everywhere.

The furniture was still there. The wicker had been replaced with plastic laundry baskets full of diapers and baby clothes, ready for folding; the brass pots had been replaced with plastic laundry baskets full of toys. A mesh playpen was now the focal point of the room, and the potpourri smell I remembered was overshadowed by the faint scent of baby poop and baby spittle. Ah, those early years! Who could forget them?

Robin sank into an armchair and I took the couch.

"Congratulations—" I started.

"After Katie was born I went back for my six-week checkup. I said, 'Doc, I need some birth-control pills.' He said, 'No, you don't, Robin. Not for another eight months.' "

"Well, they say it's best to get it all done at once," I tried.

She glared at me. I shrugged. "How's Katie?" I asked.

Robin's face lit up. "She's wonderful! It's not the babies I mind, E.J., it's this damned pregnancy crap!"

I tried to hide my shock. The Robin I'd known prior to pregnancy had been a giggly, butter-wouldn't-melt-in-her-mouth type who dotted the "I" in her name with a heart and lived for the release of the newest Martha Stewart book. I don't think I'd ever heard her use a word as harsh as "crap."

"Every woman I talk to says how pregnancy was just

so wonderful!'' Robin said. ''How they felt alive with life and glowed and all that crap! Well, E.J., I don't glow! I swell! My feet, my hands! I've got hemorrhoids!'' At this she burst into tears.

I moved to her chair, sitting on the arm, and put my arms around her. She buried her face in my stomach and sobbed while I commiserated. ''I know, Robin, believe me, I know! The only good thing about pregnancy I saw were those wonderful vitamins they give you. My nails never looked better.''

She looked up at me, her face wet with tears. ''My hair's real shiny,'' she said.

I touched it. ''I know! It looks great. You're letting it grow out?''

''So I can just pull it into a ponytail and don't have to dick around with it.''

I almost laughed at her language but decided it wouldn't be the wisest course of action. ''Well, it looks wonderful. Do you know if this one's a boy or a girl?''

Bad question. She burst into tears again. Through her sobs, she said, ''I don't know! But I want another girl! I know that's selfish, but that's what I want!''

''Honey, it's okay! You can want another girl!''

''Keith wants a boy!'' she sobbed.

I patted her shoulder some more. ''Katie will be thrilled no matter what it is,'' I told her. ''Either a baby sister to play dolls with or a baby brother to bully. She'll love it.''

Robin brightened. ''She's going to be a wonderful big sister,'' she said.

I grinned. ''If you need any help dealing with sibling rivalry, don't call me,'' I said. ''We still haven't worked that out yet.''

Robin dried her face on the hem of her maternity top, trying to pull herself out of the chair. ''I'm sorry, E.J., I haven't offered you anything—''

I stood up. ''Stop. We're going to pretend we're in my house, and I'm going to wait on you. Robin, would you like some tea?''

"Decaffeinated. It's in the—"

"I'll find it."

She watched while I moved into the kitchen area of the great room, homing in on the tea bags like a sailor to a bar after a long sea voyage. I put water on to boil in the kettle and found two mugs. "Honey, sugar, or substitute?" I asked her.

"One sugar and a touch of milk," she said, leaning back in the chair, her feet up on the ottoman, watching me with a relaxed look on her face. "Do you do windows?" she asked.

"Not even my own," I answered.

I made the tea, found some butter cookies in the Cookie Monster jar, and brought everything out to where Robin sat.

"I suppose I should ask what you're doing here," Robin said, sipping her tea, "but you might tell me and then expect to be able to leave."

"I have a while, Robin," I said, smiling, "and we should probably talk about life a little."

Which we did. She told me all the joys of Katie, and I tried to put a positive spin on the antics of my own offspring. We discussed how turned on Keith got by Robin's pregnancy (a thought I'd just as soon not know about my personal spiritual leader), and how Willis had spent each of our nine-month periods staring at the car as a means of escape. We talked about how cute Antonio Bandaras was and whether or not Madonna would have another baby. We discussed cloth versus disposable, and public versus private kindergarten.

Finally, I got a chance to ask what I'd come for. She told me about an interdenominational conference Keith was trying to organize for the tricounty area.

"I just met a minister in Swamp Creek," I said. "I wondered if Keith knew him. Rice Albany from the Almighty Christ Redeemer Basic Bible Church?"

Robin almost spit her last sip of tea across the room. "How in the world did you meet that nincompoop?"

Nincompoop? I thought. I hadn't heard that word since grammar school. I told her briefly about my friendship with Brenna and her grandmother.

"I can't say I was terribly impressed with Brother Rice," I said, giving her the lead.

"That's because you're a good judge of character, E.J." She looked around the room to make sure we were alone. As far as I knew, Katie would have been our only witness and, by the baby monitor on the coffee table, she appeared to be still asleep. "I think he's a con artist," she whispered.

I nodded my head. "Well," I said. And let it go at that.

"He showed up in Swamp Creek about a year ago, just after the Baptist church there burned down. They only had a lay preacher and he got transferred by his company so there was nothing at all in Swamp Creek and the people were going to have to scatter to Black Cat Ridge and Codderville. And then up jumps Rice Albany!" She wiggled her eyebrows at me.

"Where did he come from?" I asked.

"Who knows? He said he had a congregation in Houston, but, just between you and me, Keith checked him out and no one in Houston ever heard of him."

"Well, Houston's a huge city, Robin. If it was some small, off-the-wall church—"

"Even the small off-the-wall ones are affiliated with something. Not Rice Albany."

"Does he have a seminary degree?" I asked.

Robin shrugged. "Not that I've ever heard of."

I told her about my visit to his place, and all the toys surrounding the modest trailer. "Sounds like the type," she said. "Instead of taking money, he just takes their possessions. Whatever is easy to move. We've seen this before in other communities. Con men like him come in, tell these poor people God wants them to give 50 percent instead of ten, or 90 percent, if they can get it. If the congregation doesn't have the cash, he'll be happy to take pink slips. Then he starts selling stuff on the sly and, when he's sucked them as dry as dust, he moves on to the next town. Sorry, I shouldn't say he. I've seen women do it, too.''

Robin was, if not confirming, at least firming up earlier thoughts on Brother Rice Albany. But how did this lead to murder?

I spent another fifteen minutes with Robin, talking trash. When Katie finally woke up, I spent another ten cooing and cuddling before taking my leave and hightailing it to Vera's house.

I was in luck. She was just pulling some banana nut bread out of the oven.

''Nothing like banana nut bread when it's cold enough outside for the oven to steam the windows,'' Vera said. ''Makes me feel all cozy.''

I slathered margarine (I know, I know) on the nut bread and told Vera what Robin had told me about Rice Albany.

''Well, he looked like a sleazy so-and-so, you ask me,'' she said. ''So how do you prove he killed Lori and David?''

I sighed. Vera truly loved her giant leaps. ''First we have to come up with a scenario that makes some sense, Vera,'' I said. ''I mean, okay, he's a con man, and he was counseling Lori. That's all we've got. And we don't even have proof that he's a con man. Just an assumption.''

''Okay,'' Vera said, warming up, ''he's counseling Lori. He lets something slip about how he's conning all those poor folks, and she tries to blackmail him—''

''How does that bring David into it?''

''Well, Lori told David when they talked on the phone—''

I shook my head. ''I'm beginning to wonder if they ever did talk on the phone,'' I said.

Vera raised an eyebrow. ''Say what?'' she said.

''Listen,'' I said. ''One: Nobody ever talked to David when he called. No one even heard the phone ring. Two: Lori said David was in Houston and they were still married. David wasn't in Houston. He was in La Grange, and if he was still married to her, well, he was committing bigamy, because he was also married to that woman in La Grange. Three—I don't have a three, but do you see where I'm going with this?''

''No,'' Vera said.

''I don't think Lori was in contact with David at all. I think it was all a pipe dream on her part.''

''Then why in the world would she torment Brenna saying she was moving her to Houston?''

I shook my head. ''I don't know. But maybe you just said it. To torment Brenna. Or maybe she thought she could find David. Start over again. I don't know!''

''Well, you don't have to get mad about it,'' Vera said.

''I'm sorry,'' I said. ''I didn't mean to raise my voice. It's all just so damned frustrating!''

''Tell me about it,'' Vera said, slicing off two more pieces of nut bread. ''But the big question is: Where's Brenna?''

We both just looked at each other. Finally, I shook my head. ''I wish I knew,'' I said.

''I called Millie Conrad,'' Vera said. ''Hasn't heard a word from her.''

''Did you call the school?''

''Didn't get a chance. They called me. Wanted to know why she wasn't in school today. Told 'em she was sick.''

''Good thinking,'' I said. ''When she comes back—''

I let the words hang there. ''When she comes back.'' Back to what?

I drove to Black Cat Ridge in time to pick up the kids, my mind occupied the entire way there with thoughts of Brother Rice Albany. How could I find out more about him? And what good would it do? Why would Lori knowing he was a con man, if she did, lead to her murder? Even if she tried to blackmail him, all he had to do was take his toys and leave. Just like he was probably planning to do anyway. There couldn't be that much more loot to get out of Swamp Creek, Texas. And even if she was blackmailing him, and even if he did kill her, how did that relate to David Tyler's murder?

Because I was convinced Lori had been lying about her contact with David. Lying to herself as well as her mother and Brenna, but lying nonetheless. And if there had been no contact between Lori and David, then there was no way he knew of Rice Albany's existence, much less his con-artist status.

Unless—*Okay,* I thought. *How's this? Brother Rice is counseling Lori, and she's telling him all about her great new love affair with her estranged husband and how they're getting back together. And then she blackmails him and tells him that her husband's in on it. So he kills Lori then goes after David—*

Who Lori thought was in Houston. So how did Brother Rice find him? I realized I was stretching credibility a bit far.

Luckily I was spared any more speculation by the arrival of my three bundles of joy jumping into the van and trying to pull each other's hair out in an attempt to ride shotgun. I settled that by making them all ride in the back.

I could have opted to be one child's special mommy of the day, but instead I went for all-out child rebellion. This could mean I wouldn't get spoken to for several hours, which isn't all that big a sacrifice. Unfortunately Megan has never been able to keep a mad going or her mouth shut for more than one minute at a time.

The phone was ringing as I unlocked the door. All three pushed over me to get to it. Graham, the oldest and therefore still the tallest, got there first.

"Aldo's Tamale House," he said in his cute little way. "Oh, hey, Grandma . . . No, it sucked as usual . . . Yeah, she's here. You wanna talk to her?" He held the phone out to me. "It's Grandma," he said.

"Vera?" I said.

"I just got a call from Brenna's friend Marty from school. You know who I'm talking—"

"Yes! What did she say?"

"Trent Mosher's run away from home."

"Who?"

"Trent! E.J.! That boy Brenna liked!"

"You think—"

"Well, it's some coincidence, girl!"

"Does Marty know anything about Brenna?"

"She called to tell Brenna about Trent. I just told her Brenna was sick and couldn't come to the phone."

"This could have nothing whatsoever to do with Brenna."

"Well, I'm just saying the timing is mighty coincidental."

"What do we do with this?" I asked.

Vera sighed. "That's why I called you! I thought you'd know!"

"Well, I don't. Let me think about it. I'll call you later."

I looked at the empty kitchen counter. I'd forgotten to put anything out for dinner. Cooking was the last thing I wanted to think about. I decided I'd wait until Willis got home from work then go to KFC for some takeout.

"And corn on the cob," Willis said from the couch.

"Okay. A ten-piece bucket, mashed potatoes and gravy, *and* corn on the cob."

"As the vegetable," he reasoned.

"Willis, corn is a starch."

"Is it not also a vegetable?"

I sighed and pulled on my jacket. "At least heat up a can of green beans, okay?"

"Why? Who's going to eat them?"

"I thought we lived in the nineties," I said. "When did we slip into the fifties time warp?"

"Corn is a vegetable," he insisted.

I slammed the back door and crossed the yard to the garage and the minivan.

The KFC was in a strip shopping center on the highway into Codderville. Black Cat Ridge's rush hour doesn't start until about six-thirty. That's because most of the working people living there commute to jobs in Austin and some as far away as Houston. Willis gets home generally around five-fifteen, which had me this day on the road to the KFC by five-thirty.

I mention the lack of rush hour traffic to explain why I noticed the car following me. It followed me from my street onto Sagebrush Trail, from there to Black Cat Ridge Boulevard, and from there it, too, took a left turn onto the highway. This is not all that unusual because anyone living on or driving through my street and wanting to go to Codderville would have taken those exact turns.

What they probably would not do is stay at such a consistent pace behind me. When I sped up, the car sped up. When I slowed down, it dropped back.

Personally, I can look at almost any Volkswagen Beetle and tell you what year it was made. But with a car manufactured after 1985, I'm at a loss. I had no idea what kind of car was following me. Except that it was red. Which I figured was not that great an idea for a tail car.

As I've mentioned, there are always options. I could lead the red car directly to the Codderville Police Department, or I could pull into the KFC, get my chicken, and hit the bozo with a drumstick if he messed with me.

With all that was on my mind, I wasn't in the mood to deal with Elena Luna and her crowd at the PD. Actually, I was pissed enough to want a confrontation. I had no idea who could be following me, but if it had anything to do with Brenna, or Lori and David Tyler's deaths, I wanted to know, and I wanted to know now.

I pulled the minivan into the parking lot of the KFC and waited. The red car pulled in next to me. It was a Chevy Citation. I know this because it said so on the back fender of the car. The windows were tinted. I sat there for what felt like an hour, but was probably more like a minute.

Finally, the driver's side door of the Citation opened and a man got out. As he neared my car, I realized it

wasn't a man. Not yet anyway. He was about sixteen—
and he drove what appeared to be a brand-new Chevy. I
rolled my window down.

"Trent?" I asked.

He scooted quickly to my opened window. I couldn't
blame Brenna. He *was* cute. "Mrs. Pugh?"

"Yes. Do you know where Brenna is?"

"Yes, ma'am. I've been following you—"

"I noticed."

"You did?" he said, his voice dismayed. "I thought I
was doing a good job—"

"You were," I assured him. "I'm just very good at
this."

"Oh," he said.

"Where's Brenna?" I asked.

"Can we leave my car here? I'll ride with you."

He moved quickly to the passenger side of the minivan,
darting furtive glances around the parking lot. I flipped
the switch to unlock the doors and he climbed in.

"Trent, what's going on?"

"Just drive," he said, keeping his eye on the parking
lot. "I'll explain when I know it's safe."

So I drove, not sure if we were in actual danger, or just
having a really grand old time.

Fourteen

Trent Mosher was about five-eleven, my height, had dark brown curly hair worn a little long, and was built like he probably played football. He had even teeth, dimples, and thick dark lashes over incredibly green eyes. And freckles on his nose. Okay, he was adorable.

But I didn't have time to speculate on his cuteness. I had Brenna to find or my family to feed—whichever came first.

"Okay, Trent," I said, once we were on the highway. "What's going on?"

"Take the FM4350 exit and turn left under the freeway."

"If you'll tell me why."

He turned and looked out the back window of the van, checked the lane next to him and the one next to me. "I'll take you to Brenna. But we have to go the long way. To lose any tail we might have picked up."

This kid had watched a little too much TV. "I don't

think we're being tailed,'' I said. ''Remember, I'm good at this.''

''Right,'' he said, his head swiveling as he checked for cars, ''but he might be better.''

''Who?'' I demanded.

''I don't know.''

I slammed on the brakes and pulled the minivan onto the shoulder of the road. ''Okay,'' I said, as the car stopped. ''I'm not going anywhere until you tell me what in the hell is going on!''

He turned in his seat and looked at me. ''Brenna trusts you,'' he said.

''I should hope so. I went to jail for her!''

''Huh?''

''You first.''

''I was coming home from ball practice yesterday down the old bridge road and I saw her car pulled over to the shoulder.''

Oh, shit, I thought. *Not the bridge again.*

''She was sitting on the bank, just staring at the water,'' he said.

''What time was this?'' I asked.

He thought for a moment. ''Around five-thirty, I think. Practice is usually over around five and I hung around with some of the guys for a little bit after that. So probably around five-thirty.''

''Okay. Keep going.''

''Anyway, she was all upset. It took me forever to get her to tell me what happened.'' He stopped, his eyes downcast. Furtively he glanced up at me. ''Do you know about Brenna's parents?'' he asked.

''Yes,'' I said.

He nodded. ''She said she went to La Grange when she found out about her stepfather living there. She said she just wanted to see him. Maybe tell him off. You know, she has no closure with what happened to her as a child.''

I could only assume Codderville High was teaching an

introductory psych course—or else he had time in his life for afternoon talk shows.

"She found out where he worked and drove over there," Trent continued. "She said she saw David right off the bat. Recognized him immediately. He was leaving the building and walking around to the back. So she parked her car and started to follow him. Then she saw someone she knew right behind him. That's when she heard the shot and just jumped in her car and drove out of town. And ended up at the bridge."

"Who did she see?" I asked.

Trent shook his head. "She wouldn't tell me. She'll only tell you. That's why I had to come get you."

I started the car and pulled onto the highway, heading for the FM4350 exit. "Did she say anything at all about the person she saw?"

He shook his head again. "No, not a thing." He looked at me. "Is she in trouble?"

"The police think she did it," I told him.

"Shit," he said, slumping down in his seat. "They're such idiots!"

At this point, I had to agree.

We were heading to Trent's dad's fishing cabin upstream on the Colorado. The cabin was for sale, and the family hadn't used it in years, so Trent thought it was a safe place where no one would think of looking.

It doesn't take long, once you're outside the city limits of Codderville, to find yourself in serious country. The farm-to-market road was dotted with an occasional farmhouse, but mostly it was fields filled with winter wheat, cattle, and new-growth trees.

After about ten miles of this, Trent instructed me to turn right toward the river. This was a hard-packed dirt road that led from fields to heavy vegetation, to large, old-growth trees overlapping the road. We turned from that onto an even smaller road, dense with trees, the dirt of the road less hard-packed and more prone to potholes and mud.

It was less than a mile down this road before we turned into the driveway of the fishing shack. It was actually more of a summer cottage, a small white-framed bungalow with a screened-in front porch and a deck on the back that I could see from the driveway. The white-painted deck stepped down to a white wooden walkway that led downhill to the dock and river, all over gently rolling St. Augustine.

There was only one problem. My old station wagon wasn't there.

"Where's her car?" I asked.

"We hid it in the bushes about a mile from here," he said. Then he walked out in the road and, standing in the mud, stared toward the bend in the road to see if we'd been followed. Satisfied, he led me to the screened-in porch. Opening the front door of the cottage, he called, "Brenna, I got her!"

There was no response.

"Brenna?" he called again.

"Brenna?" I called.

There was no answer. Trent tore through the house, opening doors, looking in closets and under beds. Brenna was not in the house. We went out on the deck and stared down to the river. She was not there.

Trent collapsed on one of the steps. "Oh, shit!" he said. "I never should have left her!"

"Trent, you said 'he.' Is that what she said?"

"Huh?"

"When you thought somebody might be following us. You said 'he.' Did Brenna indicate to you that whoever it was she saw was a man?"

He hunched his shoulders in thought. Then shook his head. "I don't know. I don't think so. I think I just used 'he' in general, ya know?"

I nodded my head. "Try to think," I said. "Tell me

exactly what she said about the person she saw following David.''

He leaned his elbows on his knees, cupping his head in his hands. "Shit, I don't know. She said . . . okay, she said she got out of the car to confront her stepdad. She said she wasn't sure where he was going, then she saw the Porta Potti. She stopped because she knew she couldn't confront him in the can, you know?''

I nodded my head.

"So she said she was thinking what to do, whether to wait where she was, or go up and be outside the door when he came out. Then she saw this someone come from the back side of the Porta Potti and they opened the front door and just started shooting.''

I held out my hand to the boy. "Come on," I said, "let's go see if her car's still where you left it.''

We got in the minivan and drove the mile down the old road to where Trent thought they'd left the car. We found the distinctive tire marks the heavy station wagon had left in the soft earth next to the road, and the inevitable oil spot, but no station wagon.

"You have to call the police," Willis said.

"I know," I said, picking up the portable phone. I handed Trent the cell phone. "Call your parents and let them know where you are and that you're all right. Now.''

"Yes, ma'am," he said, taking the phone from my hand.

I dialed Luna's number at the police station. She wasn't in. I called the number for the house next door.

"Hello?''

"Luna, it's me.''

Silence greeted me.

"I think something bad could be happening to Brenna. I need your help.''

"Where is she?''

"I don't know—''

"I've heard this before!''

"I know where she was two hours ago. If you're interested, get your ass over here." I hung up the phone. With Luna it's always best to be the first one playing the assertive bitch.

Trent was telling Luna the story he'd told me earlier when Willis went to the door to answer the bell.

I followed my husband. He opened the door and stared at the man standing there. "Willis?" the man said.

"Jim?" Willis said. "Shit! How you doing?"

"Well, not great. I understand you have my kid here."

"Trent's your kid? Well, duh, of course." Remembering me, Willis put his arm around me and said, "Jim Mosher, my wife E.J. Pugh. E.J., Jim and I played ball together in high school. Best quarterback the team ever had."

"Nothing works without a good running back, ma'am," Jim said, grinning. "And I had the best."

"Trent's in here," I said, hoping to put a quick end to the macho reunion.

Trent stood up when his father entered the room. "Dad," he said.

The look on Jim Mosher's face I'd seen on Willis's face, my face, the face of every parent who'd been through hell over a child—which is to say, every parent, period. His face showed anger, relief, happiness, all sharing space in a single look. Jim had his own options: reprimand, punishment, or go with his gut.

He went with his gut. He took his son in his arms and hugged him hard. Gently I heard him say, "I'm gonna kill you!"

"I'm okay, Dad," Trent said. "And I'm sorry, but I had to do it."

So we all sat down and Trent told his story once again. While the men were discussing it, I motioned for Luna to join me in the kitchen.

"What?" she said. She still wasn't happy with me, but then, I really didn't care.

I told her my theory about Lori and David Tyler.

"Already checked it out," Luna said. "You see, I'm a detective with a legitimate police agency. Therefore, I have access to official files and information. Would you like me to explain how it works?"

"What did you find out?" I said, trying to ignore her.

She rested an ample hip on the breakfast room table. "David Tyler officially divorced Lorabell Tyler in 1989. He and Martha Lynn Morris were married in June of 1990. She had one child from a previous marriage, and she and David have had two children together. According to the records at the Huntsville Women's Penitentiary, the only record they have of any visitors for Lorabell Tyler, other than her lawyer and the chaplain, were two visits from her mother, one in early 1989 and another in 1992. Both around the date of Lori's birthday. David Tyler never visited her in prison. Ever."

"Phone calls? Letters?"

"The divorce papers were the only correspondence she received from him. She got some cards and a couple of letters from her mother, and her Publishers Clearing House Sweepstakes, but that was about it. The only phone calls were once a year Christmas Eve calls from her mother."

I sank down on the chair. Poor Lori, I thought. Nine years in prison, no visitors, no phone calls, no letters. Nothing. Just romantic fantasies about a man who had killed her child and then dumped her. I think Lorabell Tyler might well have been the most pathetic creature I'd ever met.

Then, within a month of release, someone kills her. Someone who probably wasn't David Tyler. David Tyler, free as a bird on a technicality, dropped his wife like a hot potato and went on to live his Middle American dream. No strings attached.

"Where's Brenna?" I asked out loud.

Luna answered. "I don't know."

"She didn't do this, Luna. I swear to you she didn't."

"Pugh." She shook her head. "E.J., listen. She's the

only person in the world who would even want to kill those two losers. Nobody else cared.''

"That's not true!'' I said, jumping up. "I cared!''

"Oh? Did you kill them?''

"No! You know what I mean! People care—''

"That's why David Tyler was able to remarry a woman with a child, father two more children? Live a nice little life in La Grange, complete with job, family, church affiliation, and a dog? Face it, Pugh. Once the sensationalism of a case like Branson McGraw's dies down, nobody gives a shit. People are drawn to child-abuse cases like they're drawn to car wrecks on the freeway. They want to watch, but they certainly don't want to clean up the mess afterward.''

"God, you're a cynic. I'd hate to live in your head, Luna.''

"Then you explain to me how society at large came to Brenna's aid after all that shit came down, okay? You explain to me how they kept her from living in virtual poverty with a mean old woman like Millie Conrad. You show me how all those caring people, yourself included, who stared at the paper and the TV every day during that trial—you show me how they helped the last little victim. Show me!''

"What did you do?'' I demanded of her.

"Nothing! That's exactly what I'm talking about! And neither did you!''

We stared at each other, drenched in our guilt. Both knowing how right she was.

It was a long, miserable night. There was an APB out on Brenna, but no one had seen her or the old station wagon. They'd both disappeared into thin air. Someone had killed two people—someone had cared enough to see them dead.

In reading about crime, in my talks with Luna, I knew there were only two reasons to murder, and they boiled down to love and money.

Lori Tyler was an ex-con with barely the clothes on her back. She had no money. David Tyler was a mechanic living in a mortgaged house and driving cars that had payments. Where's the money? Answer: Nowhere. Money wasn't the issue in this case.

Love? Well, love encompasses a lot of things, including hate, revenge, retribution, jealousy.

How right was Luna? Did anyone else care enough to kill those two? Was Brenna the only one hurt by them? The only one who would want retribution?

What about Branson Lee's real father, Larry McGraw? Where was he?

There was a slight resemblance between the picture of Larry McGraw taken sixteen years earlier and the man I'd seen in confrontation with Lori Tyler shortly before her death. The man who called himself Rickie Brooks, who said he was a neighbor from the Tyler's Cypress-Fairbanks days.

Brenna didn't recognize Rickie Brooks and rarely spoke of her natural father, Larry McGraw, except in remembering the time her mother held her close while Lori waited to have her wounds healed—wounds inflicted by Larry McGraw. Would this battering ex-husband kill in retribution for a son he had never known?

Lori left him shortly after she found out she was pregnant. There was a good chance he didn't even know about his son.

Or maybe he didn't know until the sensational trial.

If that was the case, if he only found out then about his son, and he felt retribution was in order, why not kill David Tyler the minute he became a free man? Why did he wait nine years?

My mind kept tickling me with the idea that there was no neighbor named Rickie Brooks; that the man who claimed that name was really Larry McGraw. But why? Why would he claim to be someone else? Why confront Lori? Why kill Lori? And if he did kill David, how did he know where he was? Lori didn't know.

Brenna had only been three years old when Lori left

her first husband. She wouldn't recognize her father after all those years. But Lori would have.

What about Millie Conrad? Surely she would have recognized the son-in-law who beat her daughter even after all these years. Rickie Brooks had been at Lori's funeral, surely Millie would have recognized him—Wait. He hadn't been in the church. He was coming from the parking lot when he approached Brenna, so there was a very real possibility that Millie Conrad had never seen him.

Could Rickie Brooks really be Larry McGraw?

Maybe someone, someone like Luna, "a detective with a legitimate police agency, therefore able to access official files and information," should find out a little something about Larry McGraw and his latest known whereabouts. And maybe check into the existence of a neighbor in Cypress-Fairbanks all those years ago by the name of Rickie Brooks.

And maybe, while she was at it, she could find out something about Brother Rice Albany of the Almighty Christ Redeemer Basic Bible Church. From what Robin Reynolds had told me, there was a good chance Brother Rice had a record.

How that connected to the murders of Lori and David Tyler, I didn't know. But if I didn't have these two—or three—to check out, I was left with Brenna. And I wasn't about to leave my speculation there.

The next morning I called Luna at the station. "Detective Luna," she said on answering her line.

"Hi, it's me," I said.

"What?"

"Have you checked out Larry McGraw?" I asked, knowing small talk would not get me anywhere with Luna at the moment.

"Brenna's natural father?"

"Right."

"No. Why should we? Remember, E.J., this isn't our case or our jurisdiction. The sheriff has Lori's case and the authorities in La Grange have David's case. We are not involved."

"All you have to do is call the sheriff and ask," I said sweetly.

"I doubt Lance Moncrief needs my help—or yours," she said.

"And while you have him on the line," I said, ignoring her, "ask him to check out the rap sheet on Brother Rice Albany, Millie Conrad's preacher."

"For heaven's sake, why?" Luna demanded.

"Because I hear from reliable, and I mean very reliable, sources that he has a record as a con artist, embezzling from church groups. And he was 'counseling' Lori Tyler after her release. There could be a connection."

There was a long silence before she said, "I'm not promising anything—"

"And is there any way you can contact the police in Cypress-Fairbanks and find out if there was a man living there when Branson McGraw was killed by the name of Rickie Brooks?"

"Jeez. What's this about?"

"I'll tell you later. Could you find out?"

"We had a drive-by shooting last night in East Codderville, Pugh. An eighty-year-old woman is in the hospital. I have other things to do, you know."

"I understand that. I'm talking a five-minute phone call here."

"First tell me why."

I sighed. The woman was *so* difficult. "There's a good chance Larry McGraw is in town and had a confrontation with Lori shortly before she died."

"What?" Luna screeched.

I held the phone away from my ear. "He's going by the name of Rickie Brooks and—"

"Then what makes you think he's Larry McGraw?"

"He looks like him."

"When did you meet McGraw?"

"I haven't but—"

"But what?" she said, her voice showing her exasperation.

"I've seen a picture."

Luna sighed. "Pugh, you are out of your ever-loving mind. You are chasing shadows to get this kid off. Wake up and smell the coffee, hon."

"Smell your own damned coffee. Just make the phone call to Cy-Fair for me! Please?"

"One call," she said. "Only one call."

I grinned to myself. "Thanks, Luna. I owe you lunch."

"No, you owe me dinner," she said, and hung up.

I sat at the table in the kitchen contemplating my next move. It would be just like Luna to find out the answers to my questions, then not let me know what they were. Meanwhile, Brenna was missing, and she could be in trouble.

The phone rang. No way could it be Luna this quick, I thought. But I hoped so nonetheless.

"Hello?" I said.

"Mrs. Pugh?"

"Yes?"

"This is Crystal Blanchard—"

"Oh, hello, Mrs. Blanchard."

She laughed, then said, "Is there any way we can get off the 'Mrs.' kick? My name's Crystal."

"Hi, Crystal. It's E.J."

"Great. Now I don't have to keep looking over my shoulder for my mother-in-law," she said. "The reason I called." She sighed. "I know I seem to keep interfering in Brenna's life, and I don't mean to. That's why I called you rather than calling back to your mother-in-law's house."

"What's wrong?" I asked, waiting for yet another shoe to drop.

"I'm sorry. Nothing's wrong. I just found out from mutual friends about David Tyler's funeral. I wasn't sure whether Brenna would want to go. I mean, I probably wouldn't, but you know what they say about closure on the 'Oprah' show—''

"When is the funeral?" I asked.

"Today at two o'clock. At the Second Avenue Baptist Church here in La Grange."

"I'm not sure Brenna would want to come, Crystal. But I'll be there," I said.

"I'll save you a seat," she said, and we rang off.

I wasn't sure why I was going to David Tyler's funeral, but there was always a chance I could learn something. There was also the outside chance Brenna might show up.

If she was okay.

If she was alive.

I pushed that thought out of my mind and decided a trip back to Brother Rice's parsonage might be in order.

I grabbed the cell phone, a fresh battery, and gave Vera instructions to call me if she heard anything from Brenna, and to pick up the kids since I would need to go straight to the funeral.

Then, of course, I had to convince her that her presence wasn't needed at David Tyler's funeral. That took about twelve dollars' worth of cell phone time.

The sky was overcast and gray, thick clouds promising something nasty, and the weatherman on my favorite radio station was proclaiming freezing rain by rush hour. I turned up the heater in the minivan and headed for Swamp Creek.

I found Brother Rice's trailer again without any trouble. Some of the toys I'd noticed on my first visit were gone, and I had to wonder if they'd been liquidated to help in Rice Albany's quick getaway from Swamp Creek.

The Good Brother Rice came to the door of the single-wide trailer as I pulled into the yard. His girth swallowed the hole of the doorway, the only light coming from the large gap between the top of his bewigged head and the lintel of the door.

As I got out of the car, he smiled and said, "May I help you?"

"Yes, Brother Rice. I'm not sure if you remember me—"

"You're little Brenna McGraw's friend."

"Yes, that's right. I was wondering if we could talk for a moment?"

"Certainly, child. I'm always there for those who need me."

Whoopee, I thought. He moved back and I entered the trailer.

The last time I'd been out here, we'd spoken in the yard and I didn't see the inside of the trailer. It was a single-wide, probably no more than one or two bedrooms, and I had to wonder how the rotund preacher made his way around inside it.

The trailer was crammed full of more loot. A dark maroon leather love seat and matching sofa formed an "L" in one corner while a huge entertainment center took up one entire wall. A big-screen TV, VCR, CD stereo system with large speakers, a camcorder, and other smaller electronics were stuffed into the entertainment center.

There were enough appliances in the tiny kitchen— bread maker, espresso machine, food processor, indoor rotisserie, etc.—to furnish a small hardware store. Gifts from a grateful congregation? Or more penance to be turned into cash for a quick getaway?

He offered me the kid leather love seat and waited for me to seat myself before sinking into the matching sofa. "It's Miz Pugh, right?" he said, smiling a full-wattage smile.

"That's right," I said.

"What can I do for you, Miz Pugh?"

"I was wondering if you might be able to help me. I understand you were counseling Lorabell Tyler before she died?"

He nodded his head. "Sister Lorabell and I spoke on a few occasions, yes."

"What exactly were you counseling her regarding, Brother Rice?"

"I'm sorry, Miz Pugh, but that was between me, Lorabell, and the Lord."

"Haven't the police asked you about this, Brother Rice?"

"I may be just a Protestant, not a heathen Catholic, but the confidentiality of the confession is the same, Little Miss," he said, glaring at me.

"I understand that, Brother Rice. But in this case, Lori is dead. You can't hurt her by answering a few questions. And I promise I won't ask anything that would break the confidentiality."

He tilted his head in what appeared to be an affirmative answer.

"Did she ever mention David Tyler?" I asked.

"Why, I believe she did, yes."

"What did she say?"

He cocked his head at me and smiled. "What is it you want to know exactly, Miz Pugh?"

I shrugged my shoulders. "I'm trying to help Brenna, Brother Rice. She could be in trouble. I know she had nothing to do with what happened to her mother—"

"It's in the Lord's hands now."

"But the Lord gave us brains to use, Brother Rice."

His smile was tight. "A very humanistic viewpoint, Miz Pugh."

"Did Lori tell you she and David Tyler were still married?"

"Why, yes, she did. She asked me to officiate when they renewed their vows."

"Would it surprise you to know that David Tyler has a wife and three children and lives in a town other than Houston?"

He cocked his head again, like a fat little bird. "Well, goodness. I would have to say yes to that, Miz Pugh."

"Where were you the day before yesterday, between four and six?" I asked abruptly.

He narrowed his eyes at me. "Wednesday? Well, now, I'm not sure. Why do you ask?"

"I'd like to establish your whereabouts at the time of David Tyler's murder," I said.

"Do what?" he demanded. "What the shit are you talking about?"

"My, my, such language from a man of God. Where were you?" I demanded.

He stood abruptly and went to the door of the trailer, opening it wide. "Get out," he said. "Now."

"You haven't answered my question, Brother Rice," I said, remaining seated. "Where were you?"

"I don't have to answer your questions, Little Miss. I want you out of here now!"

"You answer my questions, or the sheriff's," I said. "I think I'd be easier to get along with."

He let the door slowly close and turned to stare at me. The look he gave me wasn't the least bit holy. "You threatening to sic the cops on me, Little Miss?"

It was at this point I realized Brother Rice Albany was between me and the only means of escape in the tiny, cramped trailer. I had, once again, painted myself into a corner.

I stood up. "Actually, Brother Rice, I've already alerted them. They're running your sheet now—"

"Well, fuck!" he said, and rushed past me into the bedroom of the trailer. I could see him through the passageway, grabbing suitcases out of the small closet and throwing them on the bed. He was busily grabbing garments from drawers while I eased my cell phone out of my purse. I hit the speed dial for 911 and asked, in a whisper, to be put through to Sheriff Moncrief immediately.

Rice Albany was in his bathroom, throwing lotions and what have you into his bag when Moncrief came on the line.

"This is E.J. Pugh," I whispered. "I'm at Rice Albany's trailer and he's getting ready to take a powder—"

"Who is this? Speak up!" the sheriff said.

Okay, great buns but bad ears. "E.J. Pugh—" I said a bit louder.

"Oh, God, not you. Look, your friend Luna called. I'm

trying to run this investigation as best I can, Miz Pugh, and I really can't put up with all the interruptions—"

"Rice Albany's packing his bags now!"

"So?"

"Sheriff—" I started, but the cell phone was grabbed from my hands.

Rice Albany began banging the phone against the kitchen counter until it shattered, making pitiful little electronic screams as it died.

Rice Albany pushed me down on the couch. "You know, if I'da killed either Lorabell or David Tyler, then killing you would be nothing, right, Little Miss?"

"Ah, I never said you killed anyone—"

"Well, I didn't. I may not be a saint, but I ain't never killed anyone. Now, if you'll help me get some of these here electronics and them motorcycles outside into the RV, I'll be on my way."

"I won't help you do diddly," I said.

"Okay, fine," he said. "See ya."

He threw his bags outside, and began gathering up electronics equipment, then he walked out of the trailer and shut the door.

I wasn't too far behind him. I tried the door but it was locked from the outside. I began to hammer on it. "Albany, let me out of here!"

I heard his high-pitched laughter out in the yard. "You shoulda helped, Little Miss!"

I kicked and kicked on the trailer door, but nothing happened. There was no phone anywhere in the trailer—except for my dead or dying cell phone sitting pitifully on the kitchen counter.

The tiny windows of the trailer were the screw-out kind and there was no way I'd get my five-foot-eleven, 175-pound frame through one of them.

I was locked in a single-wide trailer in the middle of nowhere. And the only person who knew I was here was Sheriff Lance Moncrief. And he hadn't seemed particularly interested.

Fifteen

I sat on the couch with my shattered cell phone and tried to put the pieces back together again. The little hooky that holds the battery in was broken off, but I found some rubber bands in Brother Rice's kitchen and managed to keep the battery in by twisting the bands tightly around it. It still wouldn't come on. I messed with it and messed with it, and finally, in my frustration, slammed it against the coffee table.

I heard a faint electronic beep and the lights shown on the switch pad. I picked it up and dialed Luna's number the long way, figuring the keyed in numbers probably weren't working now. The phone on the other end rang in a disjointed sort of way. Naturally, I got her voice mail.

I carefully hung up and dialed Vera's number. Thankfully, she picked up on the first ring.

"Hello?" she said.

"Vera it's me—"

"Hello?" she said.

"Vera!" I yelled loudly. "It's E.J.!"

"Hello? Is anyone there?"

"VERA!!!" I screamed.

"Who's that?" she yelled back, hurting my ear.

"VERA! IT'S E.J. CAN YOU HEAR ME?"

"E.J., is that you?"

"YES! CAN YOU HEAR ME?"

"Just barely, hon. Speak up!"

"I'M LOCKED IN BROTHER RICE'S TRAILER!"

"You're trailing Brother Rice? Where's he going?"

"NO! VERA, LISTEN! I'M LOCKED IN HIS TRAILER!"

"You're going to the trailer? What for?"

"LISTEN!! I . . . AM . . ."

"You are . . ."

"LOCKED . . ."

"Locked?"

"IN."

"In . . ."

"BROTHER RICE'S . . ."

"Brother Rice's . . ."

"TRAILER!"

"Trailer. Oh. Oh! You're locked in Brother Rice's trailer?"

"YES!!!"

"Well, how in the world did that happen?"

"VERA!! COME GET ME!!"

"Come get you?"

"YES!!"

"Well, honey, I would, but I don't know where it is!"

I threw the cell phone across the room and slumped on the kid leather sofa. Frustrated beyond belief. So I went into the kitchen. Luckily, Brother Rice had my kind of sweet tooth. There was a bag of miniature Snickers Bars in a cabinet. I took them and a beer out of the refrigerator and went to the living room. I might as well get comfortable.

I'd barely finished the bag of Snickers when I heard a

horn honking outside. I ran to the window and saw Vera's old Chrysler pulling into the yard. She got out of her car and came to the door.

I yelled at her through the window. "It's locked! You'll need to get something!"

She gave me a look then pulled a board out from under the jammed door. The door opened.

"Wasn't exactly locked," she said, as I bailed out of the trailer.

"Well, it worked as well as a lock." I put my arms around her and hugged her. "Thanks," I said.

She backed away and waved her hand at me. "Don't get all mushy on me, girl," she said, clearly embarrassed. "So tell me what happened."

I did.

"I don't think he killed them," I said.

"Why not?" she demanded.

"Because if he'd killed them, he wouldn't have hesitated in killing me."

"Except the sheriff knew you were here, and I knew you were coming here. And Rice Albany knew the sheriff knew you were here, right?"

I considered it. "Yeah, he did."

"So somebody needs to put an APB out on this scumbag," she said.

"Are they playing 'Hill Street Blues' reruns on cable again?" I asked.

"Don't be fresh," she said. We made our plans quickly, then Vera said, "Let's roll—and y'all be careful out there!" Then, of course, she giggled.

We headed to our cars, both with a mission.

Vera was headed to Jim Bob Honeywell's office. From there she would call a den mother to pick up the kids from school, then she and Jim Bob would head to the sheriff's office to insist on an APB for Rice Albany.

Meanwhile, I went home, changed quickly into my black wool dress that would need to go to the cleaners soon if I kept going to funerals, and headed for David Tyler's funeral. Three funerals in not quite as many weeks was a little much; even Vera didn't attend them that regularly.

The Second Avenue Baptist Church in La Grange looked like a church, rather than a former retail establishment. It was white, had a steeple, doors, and people. Nifty.

I was a few minutes late and sneaked inside, taking a folding chair in the back. I was surprised at the number of people in attendance. Had he been that popular—or had the people of La Grange found out who had been hiding in their midst and come to see if the monster was really dead?

It was handled quickly and we were walking out the doors in less than half an hour. The new Mrs. Tyler was standing in a receiving line. I waited until near the end then went up to her.

"Mrs. Tyler," I said. Then thought, *What now?* "Sorry for your loss"? Somehow it didn't seem appropriate.

She balked when she saw me. "Oh, my God," she said. "What are you doing here?"

I swallowed and said the words. "I'm sorry for your loss."

"No you aren't!" she said, tears stinging her eyes. "You know where that bitch is who killed my husband, don't you? Tell me where she is!"

"Brenna McGraw didn't kill your husband," I said.

"She was always such a spoiled little brat," Mrs. Tyler said. "Her and her brother both!"

I shook my head in wonder. "Who told you that? The man who killed her brother?"

"It was an accident!" she said, her voice shrill.

"The police found the blanket with the tape on it, Mrs. Tyler. There was no accident."

"Get out of here!" she said. "You get out of here! And if you know where that bitch is, when they find her I hope they throw you both in jail to rot!"

I turned and walked away, wondering what had possessed me to come here. I had no right to interfere in this woman's grief, even if it was grief over a child murderer.

I was heading to the minivan when I saw him. Tall, thin, extended Adam's apple. "Larry McGraw!" I yelled.

He didn't turn around.

"Mr. Brooks!" This time he did turn around. *Damn, he's good,* I thought.

But when he saw me, he turned back and walked briskly to a car and jumped in, starting it quickly and peeling rubber out of the church parking lot. A couple going toward their car had to jump out of his way to keep from being hit.

Why was Rickie Brooks running from me?

I hopped into the minivan and took off after him. I thought maybe I'd like to find out.

I lost him. Somewhere halfway between La Grange and Codderville, on an old farm-to-market road I didn't know, he disappeared. I got stuck behind a farmer in a tractor pulling a wagon full of hay, with two cars coming in the other direction. By the time I got around the tractor, Rickie Brooks—or should I just go ahead and say Larry McGraw?—was gone.

There were three dirt roads he could have taken. I tried one, then the other. By the time I got back to the farm-to-market after checking out the second dirt road, twenty minutes had elapsed from the time I'd lost him. Wherever he was, he was long gone now.

I took the farm-to-market in the general direction of Codderville. Five miles later I changed direction. I passed a sign that said, "Swamp Creek 15 miles."

I had a new mission.

I was going to tackle Millie Conrad and Josh Morgan, in that order, to see if either had heard anything from Brenna.

Millie Conrad was home when I got there, and not particularly happy to see me. She wouldn't open the door enough to let me in, but kept the chain on and peered at me through the small crack.

"What do you want?" she demanded.

"Have you heard from Brenna?" I asked.

"And what if I have? You think you're so smart, and you lost her! And she's running around killing more people and blaming it on everybody and their brother!"

"She's been here?" I demanded. "When?"

"Couple of hours ago, give or take. I told her in no uncertain terms I didn't truck with the Devil and she wasn't setting foot in this house! I fed that girl for nine long years, put a roof over her head, clothed her—"

"She's in danger!" I screamed. "You wouldn't let her in?"

Millie Conrad snorted. "Danger, my Aunt Fanny! The only danger around here is from that she-devil child! I think David didn't beat her near enough when she was little! I know I certainly didn't!"

I stood back from the door, afraid of what I might do if I got too close to her. "There's a special hell for people like you," I said. "Be sure to say hello to your daughter and David when you get there!"

I turned and fled for the minivan, leaving a sputtering Millie Conrad behind me.

I drove as quickly as I could to Codderville and the Family Counseling Clinic. I didn't know if Josh Morgan would have time for me, but I was afraid he was just going to have to find it. I felt like my mind was shattering into a million pieces, and I'd never felt such animosity for anyone as I felt for Millie Conrad.

Lori had been pitiful, David repugnant. But Millie Conrad was evil. Maybe because Lori and David were both dead, it was easier to make Mrs. Conrad the personification of all that was wrong with the world—

Who said she was at the store when Lori died? And where was she when David was shot in the Porta Potti?

But why? Why would Millie Conrad kill the one person she professed to love? Her daughter. Why? Why? Why?

I pulled into the parking lot of the Family Counseling

Clinic and parked, jumping out of the minivan and going quickly inside.

No one was at the reception desk. The whole place was deathly quiet. I walked down the hall to Josh Morgan's office and listened at the door. There were no sounds of a counseling session going on inside. I rapped twice and opened the door.

Josh was standing in the middle of the room, pulling a T-shirt over his head. The door opening unexpectedly startled him so much his head got stuck in the armhole of his T-shirt.

"Josh, I'm sorry," I said, rushing over to help him.

I couldn't help noticing he was a lot more buff than he looked clothed. I tried not to stare at the rippling muscles of his back, or the little round scars, like large chicken-pox scars, on his back.

He pulled the shirt down and turned. "E.J.! Did we have an appointment?"

"No, I'm sorry to burst in on you like this, Josh! I just don't know what to do!"

I sat down abruptly in one of his visitor's chairs, and he moved to his chair.

"Any word on Brenna?" he asked me.

"No! And I'm at my wit's end!" I told him about my encounter with Millie Conrad. "I swear, Josh! The woman is evil! Somebody is trying to hurt Brenna, and she wouldn't even let her in the door!"

"It's unfortunate we can't pick our families," Josh said.

"Not in this case. Not anymore. Brenna has picked her family. Mine! And as soon as I find her, and as soon as all this is behind her, she'll be happy. I promise you that."

Josh reached across the space between us and touched my hand. His smile lit up his face. "I know that. Those people will never hurt her again."

I vented for half an hour, but knew I had to keep going. I had to find Brenna.

I got up and gave Josh a hug. "Thanks for being here, Josh," I said.

"I'll always be here for you—and for Brenna. She has to know that, E.J."

I smiled. "She does, Josh. I know she does."

I walked out to the parking lot feeling better. This was fixable. Brenna hadn't committed these crimes, and we would prove it. We'd find out who did. And then she'd come back to Vera's, be a part of our family, pass her SATs, go to UT, stay with us on the weekends. In a few years, Willis would give her away at her wedding, and I'd be a faux grandma at barely forty—

The parking lot was muddy from the rain earlier in the day. And empty except for my car. If the sun hadn't broken through at that moment, I might not have seen it. But it did. The sun broke through, and I saw it. Tire marks. Distinctive tire marks. Three regular tires, one with no tread, and one little mark made by a donut tire. I stepped over the marks to the middle of the space and squatted down as best I could in my wool sheath, running my fingers through the mud.

Oil. Definitively oil.

Brenna had been in this parking lot. And not very long ago.

I hopped in the minivan and hightailed it out of the lot.

I found her. Three blocks away, parked in the driveway of an empty house for sale. She was parked with the nose of the car facing the street. I pulled the van in, blocking her escape, and jumped out.

She saw me and bailed out of the car. I started to yell at her, thinking she was running from me, but instead, she ran into my arms.

"Where have you been?" she cried.

I pushed her away to look in her face. "Where have I been?" I demanded. "Where have you been?"

"Trying to find you!" she said.

"I was trying to find you!" I said.

"I keep calling you but you never answer the phone—"

"There were no messages on the machine—"

"Gawd, like I'm gonna leave a message! And your cell phone's never on—"

"Why did you leave the cabin? Trent found me—"

"I got scared! He was gone nearly all day!"

Brenna looked beyond me and grabbed my arm. "Oh, God, he's on the move again!"

"Who?" I demanded.

"Josh!"

"What are you talking about?" I asked.

She ran for the station wagon, screaming at me to move the van.

"Get in the van!" I yelled back.

She changed direction and jumped into the passenger seat.

"Follow him!" she said. "Hurry!"

I backed out of the driveway and turned the car in the direction Josh's car was moving.

"Why?" I asked.

"I saw him shoot David," she said.

I involuntarily slammed on the brakes. "What?"

Brenna moved toward me, slamming her foot on mine on the accelerator. "Don't stop! We have to keep him in sight!"

I shoved her foot away and hit the gas. "Josh? Brenna, are you positive?"

She gave me one of her looks. "Yeah, I guess I know the man I've been spending almost every afternoon with for the last two months when I see him, E.J. Please!"

"You saw him shoot David? Why didn't you go to the cops?"

"Like they'd believe me? They think I did it! And Josh knows so much about me, he could twist it to look any way he wanted!"

"But why? Why would he do it?"

Brenna shook her head. "I don't know. I just wish I knew where he was going now."

"Then you think he killed Lori, too?"

"Well, duh," she said.

"Why kill both Lori and David? I don't understand—Unless—"

"What?" she said.

My mind was teaming with activity. Thoughts were bubbling up faster than a teakettle on super boil.

"How would he know where David was?" I asked, taking a corner at about forty miles an hour, wincing as my bald tires screeched.

"Because I told him!" she said. "When I left Miss Vera's house, I went to his office. I was really freaked. I tried to tell him how I felt, but all he wanted to know was where David was. I didn't know exactly, just that he was in La Grange. I guess he followed me from Mrs. Blanchard's house to David's job." She shook her head. "That's all I can think of."

"What did you tell him? When you were in his office?"

"I don't know! That David was closer than I thought. That I thought he was going to come get me, make me live with him again—"

"Right before Lori died—you told him that Lori was taking you to Houston, right?"

"Yeah—"

"Oh, God," I said.

"What?" Brenna demanded.

We had turned on the road that led to Swamp Creek.

I knew where Josh Morgan was headed. I had told him where to go.

He was going to kill Millie Conrad.

"Get my cell phone out of my purse!" I told Brenna. "Call 911! Tell them your grandmother's address! He's going after her!"

"Oh, my God," Brenna breathed, grabbing in my purse for the cell phone. "What the hell?" she said.

I stole a quick glance, then remembered the shape of the cell phone. No way 911 could interpret what we needed them to know.

We were nearing Swamp Creek. There was a small grocery store on the corner. I slammed on the brakes. "Get out!" I yelled to Brenna. "Call 911. Tell them!"

I shoved her out the door and hit the gas. I knew no one would get there in time. Except me.

Josh's car was just pulling into Millie Conrad's driveway when I turned onto her street. I floored the minivan, hitting seventy as I swung the car into her yard, coming to an abrupt halt.

Josh stopped, staring at me. I bailed out of the car.

"Josh, no!" I said.

"E.J., get back in your van. Go back to your house."

"You're making everyone think Brenna did it! Why? How is that protecting her?"

"They have no proof," he said. "It'll never get past a grand jury. Go home, E.J."

"No, Josh," I said, stepping in front of him. "I won't let you kill anyone else."

He looked at me from his great height, his sad Herman Munster face looking into mine. "Why not? You said it yourself, E.J. The woman is evil. What she said to you—about beating Brenna? She'd do it again if she could."

"You killed Lori and David to keep them away from Brenna. Millie doesn't even want her. She wants her to stay with me, Josh. There's no way she'd take her back even if Brenna wanted to—which she doesn't. There is no threat from Millie!"

"She should be punished for what she did—"

I touched his arm, the arm that held a gun in it, pointed vaguely at Millie Conrad's house. "No, Josh," I said. "You did what you had to do to protect Brenna, I understand that. But this isn't protection, Josh, this is retribution."

"She hurt her again today. You told me so. Brenna was in danger, and she wouldn't let her in the house!"

"I was wrong, Josh. Brenna wasn't in danger. I thought she was in danger from the person who killed Lori and

David. But that person was you, and you wouldn't hurt Brenna, so she wasn't in danger, right?''

Confusion played across the large-featured face. "Yes, but—''

"So it doesn't matter what Millie Conrad did or didn't do. She's irrelevant, Josh. She's no longer a part of the picture. It's Brenna and my kids and Willis and Vera and me. And you. We're the family now, Josh. And we'll make sure Brenna's happy. Millie Conrad doesn't even exist in our family—''

It was working. I knew it was working. The arm had gone limp, no longer pointed at the house. It would have worked. Except Millie Conrad took that moment to pop out the front door.

"What are you people doing in my yard? Get out!'' she screamed, her voice a high screech. "Get out!''

Startled, Josh raised the gun. Millie saw it and began screaming. I grabbed his arm, and the gun went off.

Sixteen

We were gathered in Vera's small living room. The kids were at Luna's house, being watched over by Luna's mom. Her English wasn't great, but it took my kids very little to understand the Spanish equivalent of "stop that now or I'll tear off your arm."

The $85,000 check had come that day and on our way to Vera's house we'd stopped and bought several bottles of champagne, some thick steaks, and all the fixings. I'd order the new washing machine tomorrow, but today, we had old scores to settle.

Willis and I, on a temporary truce, sat together on the love seat, Brenna, Vera, and Jim Bob sat on the couch. Luna had pulled in kitchen chairs for herself and Sheriff Moncrief.

Sheriff Moncrief looked at Brenna. "Honey, I gotta ask: Why did you lie about the time you left school the day Lorabell was killed?"

Brenna shrugged. "I didn't lie by much," she said. "I left school a little earlier is all."

"Where did you go?" I asked.

She looked down at her lap. "No place special," she said.

"Brenna—" I started.

She sighed. "To the river. To the bridge on the Old Brenham Highway."

"Honey—"

"Everything was just so awful then, E.J. I'd told you the night before that I was thinking of running away, but the more I thought about it, the more I knew I had no place to run to."

"Were you thinking of jumping?" Luna asked in her blunt fashion.

Brenna looked at her. "Yeah, at first. But then I couldn't help remembering E.J. jumping in after me that time." She laughed. "That was the silliest thing I ever saw."

"Thanks bunches," I said.

"You looked like a great big bird flying down on top of me," Brenna said, giggling.

"That's the thanks I get—"

"For saving my life twice," she said. "At least twice. I didn't jump the second time because I got to laughing so hard thinking about you that I couldn't see where to jump."

"Serious PMS," I said.

"So then you drove back to your grandmother's house?" Lance Moncrief asked.

Brenna nodded her head. "Yeah, and saw Grandma coming the other way, so I waited for her." She shook her head, a disgusted look on her face. "I know what she told Miss Vera, but I know she saw me pull in the driveway! She was just lying!"

"Okay," Vera said, "what happened with good old Brother Rice Albany?"

Lance Moncrief had the grace to blush. "Well, now, ma'am. We don't rightly know. He could be in another state by now. But if he's still in Texas, we'll find him, and when we do they'll be a few charges. More, if Miz E.J. Pugh here is willing to press a few.''

"Like kidnapping?" I asked, hopefully.

Lance shook his head. "Now, seems to me you went willingly into his house, Miz Pugh. But reckless endangerment for starters.''

"You give me charges, Sheriff," I said, "and I'll press them.''

"Did you find out anything about the so-called Rickie Brooks?" Willis asked Luna.

"Well, E.J. getting his license plate helped a lot. And E.J., you're not gonna be real happy to hear this, but the man's name is Richard Andrew Brooks. For real. And he and his ex-wife and kids used to live next door to Brenna and the Tylers when they lived in Cypress-Fairbanks.''

"Get out of town," I said.

"I talked to his wife on the phone. She still has the house in Cy-Fair. She divorced him because—" Luna quickly looked at Brenna.

"Go ahead, Elena," she said. "You can't tell me anything about my family that's any worse than what I already know.''

"Well, she divorced him because your mom complained to her that he wouldn't leave her alone. She went to bed with him once, according to Mrs. Brooks, when Lori and David were having some marital problems, and then Rickie wouldn't leave her alone after that. Mrs. Brooks said she threw his ass out about the time Branson was killed.''

"Have you talked to him?" I asked her.

"Just in passing. He heard she was being released from prison and moving back home with her mom, and came here to see if they could start back up. He said she wasn't very interested.''

"I'd say that was an understatement, if what I saw at the Burger Hut was any indication," I said. "So I was wrong about Larry McGraw.''

"Pretty much," Luna said.

"So then why did Rickie run from me?" I asked.

"When?"

"At David Tyler's funeral."

Two voices, both loud, one belonging to my husband, the other to Brenna, said, almost in unison, "What were you doing at David Tyler's funeral?"

Luna and I both ignored them. "Oh, that," she said, breaking into a grin. "He mentioned the crazy redhead that kept bugging him. I think you made him a trifle nervous."

"By the way, Brenna," Sheriff Moncrief said, "I found out where your real daddy is, if you're interested."

Brenna made a "humph" sound, much like Vera's favorite reproving noise. "I couldn't care less," she said.

"Well, I want to know," I said. "Where is he?"

"St. Louis, Missouri," Lance said. "In the hospital. Seems he tried his abusing routine on his current girlfriend, and she managed to grab a baseball bat and beat the ever-loving crap out of him. He'll be limping for a few years to come."

"Couldn't happen to a nicer guy," his daughter said.

The woman in the easy chair, who'd been quiet up to that point, cleared her throat. We all turned to look at Anne Comstock, our family counselor and the person who had recommended Josh Morgan to us in the first place. And the reason we had gathered together at Vera's house.

"I'm so sorry," Anne said to Brenna.

"It's not your fault," Brenna said. "You didn't know."

Anne shook her head. "You're right, I didn't know. But that doesn't stop me from feeling guilty."

Anne had just come back from two hours in the La Grange jail cell of Josh Morgan.

"So what did you find out?" I asked.

Anne pulled her feet up in the chair, her arms folded across her chest. From several years of therapy with the woman I was able to recognize defensive body language when I saw it.

"I found the adoption records before I spoke with Josh, but he confirmed what I found. Josh was adopted when he was ten years old. Prior to that his name was Joshua Abraham Aycock.''

''Aycock?'' Sheriff Moncrief said. ''Like in Basil Aycock?''

''Not an easy name to forget, huh?'' Anne said.

''Who's Basil Aycock?'' I asked.

Willis touched my arm. ''You had your fascination with the Tyler stuff in Houston. For the people around her it was the Aycocks.''

Anne nodded her head. ''It all came to a head in 1968. Basil Aycock and his family lived on a farm on the road to Brenham. One afternoon, he came out of the fields, took an ax out of the shed, went into the house, and killed his wife and two of his three children. The third one was at school that day, which was rare, according to the school. Little Joshua Aycock missed a lot of school, what with broken arms, concussions, you name it.''

''Oh, my God,'' I said.

Brenna reached across the space between us and took my hand.

''Josh came home to find the carnage. He was nine years old. He heard a noise, turned, and saw his father coming after him with the ax. Basil Aycock had a lot of guns in the house. Josh grabbed a shotgun, knowing it was loaded, and blew his father's head off.''

We were all silent for a moment, thinking of that small boy with the great big guilt to bear.

''Those scars you saw on his back, E.J.?'' Anne said.

I nodded.

''They weren't chicken pox. They were cigarette burns. Apparently one of Basil Aycock's fun little games with his children.''

Brenna let go of my hand and crawled between Willis and me on the love seat. She nestled between us, protected.

''He was adopted by the Morgans, a couple in Austin. I think he would have been okay, except the similarity between—''

''He wouldn't have been okay, Anne,'' Willis said.

"Some people can deal with it. The strong ones. Like Brenna here. But he went off. It would have happened eventually. Somewhere, sometime, there would have been a client who reminded him."

Anne nodded her head. "I know you're right. I just—"

"Feel guilty?" I said.

She nodded.

"What did he say when you talked to him?" Brenna asked.

Anne smiled at the girl. "First he wanted to know how you were—physically and emotionally. He wanted me to tell you that he thought he was doing the right thing—the thing he wished someone had done for his family."

Brenna shivered under my arm. "I guess I hated them both—Lori and David. But I didn't really want them dead." She shook her head. "Maybe I did, at some point. You know, wish them dead."

I squeezed her shoulders. "Honey, we all wish people dead occasionally—"

"Yeah," Vera chimed in, "I can betcha a dollar to a donut E.J.'s wished me dead a couple of hundred times!"

"Well, it's been a while," I said, smiling at my mother-in-law. "But there was a time—"

"How's old Millie holding up?" Vera asked.

"She'll live," Luna said, her voice making it evident it made no difference to her either way. "She'll just have more to bitch about because her arm's going to let her know when it's gonna rain."

"Is it true she's suing the city?" Brenna asked Jim Bob.

"Yes, little lady, that is true. I wouldn't take the case myself, being too personally involved," he said, looking into my mother-in-law's eyes. "But she stands to make a small fortune off the city because the Family Counseling Clinic was city-run."

"It's not their fault," Brenna said.

"No, honey, it's not. And if your grandmother makes one red cent off the city, I'll be sure to put an estoppel on it since half of any money she receives should come to you."

"I don't want it," Brenna said peevishly. "I plan to earn my money."

Jim Bob smiled. It was a nice smile, with just a bit of a shark's bite to it. "We'll see," he said.

"Well, I think it's time to talk about those steaks," Vera said, pushing herself up from the sofa. "Now I do believe it's a male rite of passage to sacrifice red meat to the barbecue gods, so gentlemen—"

The men gathered in Vera's backyard to argue over the placement of charcoal briquettes, while the women gathered in the kitchen, making salad and baking potatoes. We opened a bottle of champagne and, with Luna's officially sanctioned okay, gave Brenna half a glass.

"A toast," Anne said, "to real mental and emotional health."

"Amen to that," Vera said, and we all clinked glasses and drank.

I couldn't take my eyes off Brenna as we moved about the kitchen, preparing the meal. She laughed at something Vera said, hugged her lightly, snapped a towel at Luna, and giggled.

She was ours. We couldn't take away what had happened to her as a child, or what she'd gone through as a teenager, but we could make sure that from this moment on she was loved. And that she knew it every day of her life.

She was ours. And we were hers.

A couple of hours later, as the last to leave, Willis kissed Brenna good night and he and his mother headed for the car for the next step in the good-night ritual. I stayed behind a moment with Brenna.

I kissed her lightly on the cheek. "I love you, kid," I said.

She cocked her head and looked at me. Her face serious. "You do, don't you?"

"What's not to love?" I said.

She grinned. "Good point."

"Good night, honey," I said, and headed for the door. Brenna grabbed my hand, "E.J. . . ."

I turned. "What, honey?"

"Thank you."

I smiled. "You're welcome."

Again I headed for the door. Behind me I heard her say, "I love you, too."

I smiled to myself and just kept walking.

Once alone in the minivan, I said to my husband, "We need to talk."

"What about?" he asked.

"About why you're still mad at me."

"I'm not mad," he said. "I've worked it all out."

"You have?" I asked.

"Yep. It's simple," Willis said. "My mother can't play with you anymore."

End of story.

E. J. Pugh Mysteries by
SUSAN ROGERS COOPER

"One of today's finest mystery writers"
Carolyn Hart

HOME AGAIN, HOME AGAIN
78156-5/$5.50 US/$7.50 Can
Romance author and amateur sleuth E. J. Pugh finds the latest
murderous mystery strikes much too close to home when her
husband Willis disappears.

HICKORY DICKORY STALK
78155-7/$5.50 US/$7.50 Can
An invisible, high-tech prankster is wreaking havoc with E. J.'s
computer, phone lines and bank account. She suspects a creepy
neighbor kid—until he turns up dead in the Pugh family car.

ONE, TWO, WHAT DID DADDY DO?
78417-3/$5.50 US/$7.50 Can
Everyone in town is stunned by the apparent murder-suicide of the
well-liked Lester family. But E. J. may be the only one in Black
Cat Ridge who believes the murderer still walks among them.